Make It Big

Inspirational and Motivational Stories of Achievers and Influencers

Make It Big

Inspirational and Motivational Stories of Achievers and Influencers

Conceptualized and Edited by
N KALYANI

PRABHAT
PRAKASHAN

Disclaimer : The views expressed in the stories by the fifteen contributing writers in this book are their own. They do not represent the views of the editor.

Published by
PRABHAT PRAKASHAN
4/19 Asaf Ali Road,
New Delhi-110 002 (INDIA)
e-mail: prabhatbooks@gmail.com

ISBN 978-93-5521-481-2
MAKE IT BIG: Inspirational and Motivational Stories of Achievers and Influencers
Conceptualized and Edited by N Kalyani

Edition
First, 2023

Price
₹ 300 (Rupees Three Hundred Only)

Printed at
Colour Business Centre, Delhi

Preface

We have all experienced issues that revolve around choices to make vis-à-vis education, career, and profession. The life choices to make. Often a straight-jacketed view of what makes for a good career choice and what is a preferred profession leads to one being pulled apart. Between ideas of what is lucrative and what is unprofitable. Between notions of what is successful and what is unsuccessful. Between perceptions of what is fashionable and what is boring. Between what one wants to do and what one is compelled to do due to various factors. One's choices are influenced by and based on such factors as family pressures, societal pulls and one's own calling.

All of these choices and thus our activities deeply affect our lives. Happiness and satisfaction, joy and contentment, these are the values we cherish in our lives. And naturally we wish to experience it in our own lives and share it with those around us through our varied activities. So that what we do can have a positive impact on us, those around us, and the society at large.

This was the genesis of the idea of bringing together the stories of persons whose life choices and life journeys are inspirational and motivational. They are persons who have undertaken paths that may be uncommon, novel, non-stereotypical, avant-garde. They may have taken their work to a different dimension, a different order, or given their work a whole new direction. They may have given a new flavour to an activity otherwise commonplace. They have striven hard to delve into their area of work because of the deep interest they have and the joy they experience in it. It may be chasing fluttering, colourful butterflies, or it may be walking in the terrains of the western ghats. It may be theatre, or it may be music. It may be architecture, or it may be economics. It may be dance, or it may be sculpting. It may be gardening, or it may be teaching. It may be with regard to the cotton that goes into clothing, or it may be in relation to the ingredients that go into cooking. It may be parenting, or it may be biking. It may be farming, or it may be counselling. Or it may be about pursuing multiple passions, or about multiskilling.

It is fifteen such stories that have been featured in this book. Stories of individuals who are highly motivated and inspired, and whose stories are highly motivating and inspiring. They are individuals whose stories fascinated me. They are individuals whose lives have influenced many directly and/or indirectly. They are influencers whose stories too can influence many.

❑❑❑

Acknowledgements

I am grateful to the fifteen contributing authors who have written, from their hearts, their stories that are so inspiring and motivating. They have taken time out from their very busy, hectic schedules to reflect, and to share their views and ideas; what their goals have been and what they wish to achieve in the future; and what challenges they have faced and surmounted. They have made this book possible, and to them I am deeply indebted.

❑❑❑

Make It
Big

Inspirational and Motivational Stories of Achievers and Influencers

Contents

Introduction

Make It Big is a collection of inspirational and motivational stories of fifteen achievers. Achievers whose lives serve to inspire and motivate others. Their stories, in their own words, have been presented here so you can get to know them up close and personal. Their aspirations and inspirations. What made them choose to do what they did. How they pursued what they pursued. What challenges they had to face. What limitations they had to overcome. These stories are about their success and about their achievements, and what gives them satisfaction. What their views are about the future. For themselves. And humanity in general. Their world view. In other words, their journey of life and their views that could serve as inspiration to others.

These are stories of being bold to do what one's heart says. Stories of being ready to be a trailblazer or a trendsetter. Of having the savvy to be a pioneer. Of being an innovator. Of making the most of the opportunities that come one's way. What stands out in these stories is the perseverance of the individuals, with a flexibility, and a readiness to be creative, and pursue new ideas. These are stories of enjoying what one does, and doing what one enjoys. Of loving what one does, and doing what one loves. These are stories of how joy, satisfaction, and excellence have accompanied the individuals in their work and life.

This book has stories that could embolden you. Stories that may encourage you. Stories that could enlighten you about avenues unknown to you, ventures you had never imagined. Stories that may let you make a fresh start. Stories that could allow you to take heart.

From the stories we may infer that each one of us has an unlimited potential. And the sky is the limit when it comes to achievement and excellence. The stories may make you sit up and take a re-look at what you are doing, at what you want to do, and pursue what you would love to do.

Each of the fifteen chapters here features one of the fifteen influencers who make up this book. Each chapter begins with a brief introduction of the person. And then follows the story that the person has penned for this book. Each of the fifteen individuals has taken time to write their story after reflecting on their life journey. Also included are some of the pictures provided by them of themselves and the work they do.

Thus has this book come about…

❑❑❑

CHAPTER 1

Chasing Jewelled Beauties on Wings

Isaac D Kehimkar

A butterfly enthusiast who has authored books on the butterflies of India as field guides, Isaac David Kehimkar is known as The Butterfly Man of India. Quitting the corporate job he secured after his graduation, he joined the Bombay Natural History Society (BNHS). His job let him pursue his interest in nature and wildlife, and he went on to retire as the deputy director of the BNHS in 2017. He has authored various nature and wildlife books besides those on butterflies. He is currently the chairman and director of iNaturewatch Foundation. He is also the consulting editor of the BNHS magazine, Hornbill. He specializes in designing and setting up butterfly parks in India.

I grew up in Govandi, near Deonar, in the suburbs of Mumbai. This was at a time when television was yet to arrive in Mumbai. My father had finally been able to buy the cottage we lived in.

The Introduction to Wildlife

It was because of my parents, who encouraged me to keep pets like cats, lovebirds, ducks and aquariums, that I got interested in nature. My dad often got pictorial books, for me, on American birds and African animals, which I really enjoyed reading. When I was in 8th grade, he gave me a camera to photograph my pet cats, and I got hooked on to the hobby of photographing nature. As children, during the summer vacations, we played cricket in the open rice fields, and in the rains, during the monsoons, my favourite season, I caught fishes and crabs with the local boys from the fishermen community (*koli*). These crabs and fishes would end up as my seasonal pets. That was how I got interested in exploring and knowing about nature. I often missed school to be in the rain catching tadpoles

and fishes. Butterflies too I chased and caught, but the real involvement with butterflies was yet to happen.

Being weak in mathematics, I could not go in for studying science after completing my schooling, though I wanted to. And so, I graduated in political science and psychology from the Mumbai University. However, my affinity towards nature remained strong as ever. Soon after graduating I got my first job of selling cosmetics with a big Indian company.

Entering the Portals of the BNHS

Nearly at the same time I got an opportunity to volunteer for an exhibition of snakes for the Bombay Natural History Society (BNHS). Subsequently, I got a job offer to work with this NGO, but the kind of salary they offered was too meager. When I shared my desire to work in the area of nature conservation with my mother, she was terribly upset, and warned me that no girl would marry me with the kind of meager salary the job offered. But my father was on my side, and managed to convince my mother that it was more difficult to get a job that would give satisfaction and happiness than get one of those jobs which gave a high salary. Money would come eventually, he opined. He reassured me to follow my heart.

And there I was in the BNHS, and right amidst the treasure of books, as a library assistant. I was lapping up as much as I could from the library, and also getting the opportunity to observe stalwarts like Dr Salim Ali, the renowned ornithologist, at work, when he visited the library. I did not interact with him much, as I was then just a newcomer, and he the president of the BNHS. But I once mustered up the courage, and complimented him that I liked his handwriting.

And what he advised me then, became the guidelines for my life. He said that he had worked hard to acquire that style in his handwriting, and advised me that I should always let the world see the best side of my work. He then went on to say that some opportunities come just once in a lifetime, and that one should give their best to it.

The BNHS was where I saw myself learning and growing, watching my role models like Dr Salim Ali, JC Daniel, and several others. I read about their exciting travels to remote corners of India as part of their study and research watching nature, and observing wildlife, and that is when, rather subconsciously, I aspired to write on nature like them, and even fantasized seeing these places. Luckily, at the BNHS I got the opportunities to travel to some of the places of my dream.

Romancing the Butterflies

While working with the BNHS, I met Bittu Sahgal, editor of the *Sanctuary Asia* magazine. The first issue of the magazine was just out when he wanted me to do a story on butterflies. While working on the story, on butterfly lifecycle, I got so fascinated with butterflies. From then on butterflies took over my life. And then began my chase after these winged jewels. Butterflies got me, or, rather, enticed me to travel to and explore the remote corners of India. It was thus that I really saw how beautiful and diverse India is. I realized that just one lifetime is not enough to see and know India. Soon after my article on butterflies was published in *Sanctuary Asia*, I got an offer from the World-Wide Fund for Nature-India (WWF-India) to co-author a book for beginners on the butterflies of India. At the time nature lovers had books on birds, animals, snakes and trees, but none on butterflies. And, therefore, the book I co-authored, *Common*

Butterflies of India (1992), became a best-selling title of WWF-India.

After Wynter-Blyth's book on Indian butterflies published in 1957, the BNHS had not brought out any book on butterflies. Possibly sensing this gap, the BNHS offered me to write a book on Indian butterflies. My idea of writing on butterflies was not to just sit in the library, and refer to other people's observations, but to actually see and experience butterflies and their habitats. Then on, my family trips too were for butterflies.

Capturing the Apollo Butterfly – On Camera

I would like to narrate what it took to photograph the apollo butterfly. This may be a sampler of one part of the kind of work I did, and enjoyed doing – chasing butterflies and photographing them. We were once at Tabo in Himachal Pradesh, one of the last villages near the Indo-China border above 10,000 feet. My eyes were searching for just one type of butterflies called Apollo. These butterflies are seen only above 10,000 feet. All of us, my wife, my son and the driver, were looking out for anything that would be fluttering around. I was with my camera, ready and cocked. Just then I spotted a whitish butterfly flying close to the ground with a slow fluttering flight. That was it. Yes, it was an apollo. I scrambled out of the car, and started to stalk the butterfly. It was flying slowly and steadily; I was sure to catch up. While I was closing in to frame it, the butterfly started ascending a nearby hill slope. I saw it slowly going uphill, but I was out of breath and just could not catch up on that hill slope. And there I lost my first chance to photograph my dream butterfly. I returned to the car totally upset.

The next year I was in the Valley of Flowers above 10,000 feet, and on the edge of the valley I saw the apollo again, on a lovely aster flower. Oh! what a perfect shot, I muttered as I slowly began my approach like a chameleon. I was near it, but just when I was about to point my camera, it took off, and to my dismay it slowly sailed downwards into the valley below. I just stood there at the edge of the valley. Cursing my luck.

But I wanted to photograph this elusive butterfly for my book. I was in Ladakh, and that was the third time I saw my prized butterfly at Khardung La pass in Ladakh at 17,500 feet, one of the world's highest motorable roads. It was fluttering along the road, and I recognized it – yes, it was an apollo butterfly. Now, desperate and excited, I quickly got out of the car with my camera out, and there I was running rather breathlessly at

17,500 feet after the apollo butterfly. I told myself I have to get the butterfly this time. While the butterfly kept on flying, and perching on the ground intermittently, I prayed that it should not fly uphill or take a dive into the valley. Then, luckily it was on the road, and I was stalking it with my head throbbing, and heart thumping against my chest as I was not yet properly acclimatized to move in the rarefied air of Ladakh. And then it finally sat in the middle of the road basking with its white wings spread out. Huffing and puffing, trying to steady myself, as I was visibly shaking, I finally got my first shot of my elusive apollo. It seemed so easy as the butterfly just basked in the Himalayan sun while I rattled off my camera on a clicking frenzy. Yes, finally I had captured the Common Red Apollo. On my camera. I had chased it for three consecutive years.

Butterfly Journeys

The real heartland of Indian butterflies is the north-eastern region of India. And that is the place for my annual pilgrimage. From Sikkim eastwards through Assam to Arunachal Pradesh, part of West Bengal, and the entire North East has more than 900 species of butterflies of the 1320 species of Indian butterflies.

Going around in the dense forests of Assam and Arunachal Pradesh in the North East is not easy as one has to try avoiding the blood-thirsty leeches, invisible nasty mites, and angry elephants. But my crazy passion for the winged jewels made me overcome all hurdles. Soon I was busy writing a book on the butterflies of India. The book took 10 years to complete. And, *The Book of Indian Butterflies* (2008), turned out to be a BNHS bestseller. That year the book broke all the sales records of the BNHS' publications.

During this chase, chasing the butterflies, I realized that India is truly a unique and diverse country with an amazing array of landscapes, people, animals, birds, insects and flowers. To really "see" India one lifetime is not enough. I stopped visiting foreign countries, as I found India having everything I wanted to see and photograph. I have seen most of India while chasing butterflies.

Besides butterflies, India's wildlife is indeed amazing with elephants, rhinos, leopards, king cobras, and tigers. India is indeed the land of the tiger, and now India is the only place in the world where you can see a tiger at a distance of 10 feet while you are in an open vehicle - the entry of this magnificent cat on the scene is just electrifying. It is quite an experience to look into a tiger's eyes. You will never be the same again. Have you ever done that?

With butterflies I arrived at my destination, and found myself. What I enjoy doing now is to share this with and inspire the younger generation. Saving nature is not just for birds and butterflies, but it is to secure our own future too. Birds and butterflies around us will tell us that all is well. The moment we stop seeing butterflies flying around, or find no birds singing, there would be something terribly wrong with the environment. And then not just us, but our next generation would be at risk. We need to handover this earth, in a good state of environmental health, to our children so they can live safe and happy.

❑❑❑

CHAPTER 2

A Steadfast Pursuit of my Passion for Music

Dr Usha Prasad

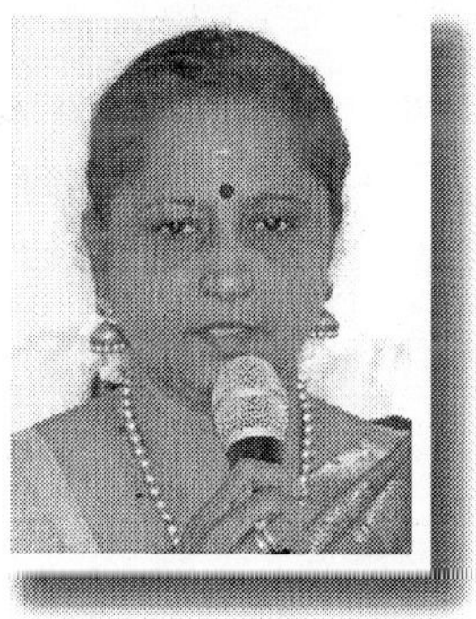

After securing a bachelor's degree in science, she turned to pursue formal education in music. She did her BA, MA and then an MPhil in Indian music. And she went on to complete her PhD in Indian music from the University of Madras in 2007. Dr Usha Prasad pursued her passion for Carnatic music with determination and perseverance. Her book, based on her doctoral research, has also been published. A multi-linguist, she has also brought out a book of the Sanskrit compositions of her music guru, the legendary Carnatic vocalist, Madurai GS Mani. The book, titled, Rājapūjita Ramyam - Stuti Gītams - Madhurai Sri GS Mani's 101 Sanskrit Compositions, was published in

2021. She has also worked as academic consultant in music composer AR Rahman's KM Music Conservatory. She now runs her music school, the Voice Academy, in Chennai.

My parents worked in the railways. My mother was the headmistress of the Railway School at Bangarapet, while my father worked as the station master, Champion Reefs, Kolar Gold Fields. I was exposed to dance and music at a very young age. My mother herself was a singer and a dancer.

Introduction to Music

I studied at the St. Joseph's Convent High School, Champion Reefs. I started learning Carnatic music from Jayalakshmi Sampath, wife of a mining engineer, who lived close to our home. We had only the manual *tambura* in class, not the *sruti* box, and so I learnt to tune the *tambura*.

Fine arts and sports were encouraged at school, and we had frequent cultural programmes. I used to learn Bharatnatyam at school. From the time I was in primary school I was exposed to listening to *harikatha kalakshepams* and music concerts. In academics I was a topper in class. I was good at sports too, and played kho-kho, throwball and field events at state level. After my 10th grade, I did my PUC, Pre-University Course, and BSc with physics, chemistry and mathematics as subjects at KGF First Grade College, Kolar Gold Fields.

We were five siblings. Amongst us, I happened to show great interest in the fine arts. In school days my father used to take me to Bengaluru to attend the Swami Chinmayananda Gita Gyana Yagna. In KGF, where we lived, *swamijis* would come every year to conduct yagnas for 15 days. At 5:30 in the morning we used to have classes on the Upanishads. In the evenings I would chant the Gita before the discourse commenced. I owe it to my father who used to drop me off for and pick me up from the programs. Around this time, I was introduced to Swami Dayananada Saraswati, while he was with the Chinmaya Mission, and became his disciple. He encouraged me to pursue music seriously. He used to have me sing before his talks in Chennai. In fact, later he paid my hostel fees when I studied music at college in Chennai, and thereafter also supported me when I pursued my PhD

As a school student I wanted to pursue medicine after my schooling, so I could become a doctor, and thus serve the people. Though I secured a seat at a medical college I had to pay a donation of Rs one lakh to get admission. As we could not afford that I opted to do a BSc course.

I graduated at the age of 17. My mother refused to let me pursue an MSc program. She feared that if I went in for higher studies, finding a matrimonial alliance for me would become difficult. Marriage right away was also not possible as I had not yet attained 18 years of age.

Pursuing Higher Education in Music

It was then that I came to Chennai to study at the Government Music College, Madras. I was directly admitted to the second of the 3-year Sangeeta Vidwan diploma course. I passed with distinction in vocal, as main subject, and veena, instrumental, as an elective subject. Thereafter I studied pedagogy in music from 1983 to 1986.

I was also introduced to the Carnatic music maestro, Madurai GS Mani, by the legendary musician, the late Salem G Desikan at Thiruvaiyaru. At that time my father used to take me to Thiruvaiyaru during the Thyagaraja Utsavam, and to Chennai during the December Music Season every year.

Mani Sir, for that is how he is referred to, initially did not want me to take up music as a profession. He advised me to join the banking service, and work as a banker. But on seeing my serious interest in music he started teaching me music. That was in the year 1983.

Later, I also started teaching, going to students' homes to take music classes. I would also send money, thus earned, to my sister and to my brother, both of whom were pursuing higher studies.

In 1987 I got married to KV Prasad, a mridangam vidwan. He used to accompany music stalwarts like Semmangudi Srinivasa Iyer, Dr M Balamuralikrishna and MS Subbulakshmi in their concerts. He used to be very busy going for the Festivals of India held overseas. He was also working in All India Radio, Chennai, as a staff artiste, playing the mridangam for film, and cassette recordings. Since he had a busy travelling schedule, I started pursuing my further studies.

Being a graduate in science, though I had a diploma in music, I could not seek admission for doing a post-graduation program in music. I, therefore, took admission to do a BA program in music, through correspondence. After completing my bachelor's, I joined the MA program in music at the Queen Mary's College in Chennai. It was my teachers who made this possible: I was sent the MA program application form and encouraged to apply for it. The classes were conveniently timed, from 10 am to 2:45 pm, so that I could drop my kids off at school, and also pick them up at school closing time. I completed my master's securing first rank.

From here there was no looking back. I joined the Madras University to pursue an MPhil program. As part of the course I studied western music, as also music in various religions. My MPhil dissertation was: *Anya-svara dhaivata* in *bhairavi*. And I was awarded a special prize for my work. Dr N Ramanathan, who was then the head of the Indian music department, was my guide.

As I had analyzed the *anya-svara* (alien note) in the *bhairavi raga* which is a *bhasanga raga*, for my MPhil dissertation, I felt I should analyze the *anya-svara* in all the *bhasanga ragas*.

The topic for my PhD therefore was: A study of *anya-svara* in *bhasanga ragas*. It was an analysis of 69 ragas, the source for the research being Sangita Sampradaya Pradarshini, a Telugu work by Subbarama Dikshitar, which contains *raga lakshanas* and notations of compositions of various composers. I did my doctoral research under my guide, Dr N Ramanathan, and lecturer, Dr RS Jayalakshmi, and received my PhD degree in 2007. My doctoral thesis was subsequently published as a book in 2019.

Pursuing higher education, and going on to successfully completing my doctoral research entailed hard work with a great deal of determination. Especially given the fact that my husband was a very busy artiste, travelling most of the time, and I had two children to bring up. I learnt to work on the computer, and would work from 10 pm to 2 am.

My mother not having let me go in for higher studies deeply affected my morale. I, therefore, determined to achieve something in my own right, to have an identity my own. I determined to become a doctorate. I owe it to my guru, Madurai GS Mani, and teachers for their encouragement, and to my family for their support.

Training with the Legendary Carnatic Vocalist Madurai GS Mani

I am fortunate to have trained in music both under the gurukulam tradition, and as part of an institution. I continue to learn from my guru, Madurai GS Mani. It has been so fruitful, and I feel blessed to be under his tutelage. I am grateful to him and his wife as I have learnt a great deal by associating with them. His knowledge in music, both Carnatic and Hindustani, as also film music, is par excellence. He used to explain the meaning of the music compositions that he taught. I am also grateful to him for the life lessons, spiritual upliftment, and noble values that he shared. My guru is practically an encyclopaedia, possessing deep knowledge be it physics, *Vedanta* or any other subject. I am proud to be his student, and to carry the legacy forward with commitment.

My book, *Rājapūjita Ramyam - Stuti Gītams - Madhurai Sri GS Mani's 101 Sanskrit Compositions*, published in 2021, is a compilation of the beautiful devotional songs composed by Mani Sir. The compositions, in praise of the divine, are rich both in content and *ragas*. *Rajapujita* is his signature in his compositions. It was my desire to make the compositions accessible to the people. And thus came the idea of publishing 101 of his compositions as the first volume of a book. This entailed learning the compositions from my guru. I would type the Sanskrit script, followed by the English diacritical script, and then the meaning and notation of the compositions in English. It was a laborious process, and took quite a few years, with my senior students too helping. It was a great learning experience. The book is my *guru dakshina* (offering to the guru) by making it available to the people. Soon I will bring out the second volume of his Sanskrit compositions.

Mani Sir has rendered his Sanskrit compositions during his concerts, and for albums. I have now started the video and audio recordings of the compositions rendered by my senior students. I wish to propagate the compositions by making them part of my performances.

Sanskrit is a beautiful, 'divine' language. Listening to and learning slokas, and the Gita, since childhood, has influenced my life. Incidentally, I am also familiar with the Kannada, Hindi, Telugu and Tamil languages. The sound vibrations of the Sanskrit language are known to impact mental and physical health. Sanskrit is one of the important languages in our music repertoire. As research scholars we were expected to know - read and write - all South Indian languages and Sanskrit; write diacritical English script, of text of other languages, and type it on the computer.

Mani Sir has also composed songs in Tamil and Telugu, and I will be bringing out, in book form, these compositions with lyric script in Tamil and Telugu respectively, and notation in English to cater to a wide audience.

Voice Academy – My Music School

I have always been passionate about teaching. The music school I run is called Voice Academy. I encourage my students to be good *rasikas* first, to appreciate music, and be proud of our rich heritage. Many of my students have become concert performers, many playback singers. My students are my extended family. I, in fact, treat them as my friends so they can approach me freely with regard to anything in their life.

In the context of appreciating music, my husband and I were particular that our children learn to appreciate music. But to have taken it as a profession has been their choice. My son, Krishna Kishor, is a global percussionist, who does live shows with leading music composers such as AR Rahman. He has now turned composer too. My daughter, Krupaa Lakshmi, married and settled in USA, is a Bharatnatyam dancer and Carnatic vocalist.

Music and More

While I sing only Carnatic music, I enjoy listening to all genres of music. I take an interest in writing articles on music, and conducting lec-dems, seminars and workshops. I also love working in the studio. I have also worked in AR Rahman's Conservatory. I enjoy activities like cooking, yoga, meditation, painting, and gardening too. These activities also help bring discipline into one's life.

I believe in Ramana Maharishi's view that what you are destined for, you will get; no one can stop it. And what you are not destined for, you will not get however much you may try.

Life is a blessing. One must feel content with and blessed for what one is. Be happy, and help make others happy. If someone throws lemons at you, make lemonade. Make the most of what you have. Take everything that comes your way as an opportunity. If one has good thoughts, good actions will follow. It is each one of us who can set an example for the next generation.

❑❑❑

CHAPTER 3

The Nomadic Journey of Learning and Wisdom

Kuntal Kumar

Kuntal Kumar did his bachelor's in hotel management from the Institute of Hotel Management, Kolkata, and an MBA from the Liverpool John Moores University, UK. A professional chef, Kuntal Kumar has worked in places world over. He started off his career in the year 1999 from Ananda in the Himalayas, near Rishikesh. He then moved to Devonshire in the UK, and thereafter came back to work in India. Subsequently he did a stint in Tanzania, and returned once again to work in India. This was followed by another overseas assignment, this time at Costa Rica. Currently he is in a project in a wellbeing retreat in the Maldives. For him it has been a culinary journey around the world. He has authored a book on

organic food titled, The Original Organic Cookbook, and is now working on his second book. He is into promoting the concepts of sustainability and the organic from the gastronomic angle.

As I was growing up out of childhood, one part of me wanted to become a soldier, another part of me wanted to become a farmer, and many little parts of me wanted to do so many different things. I grew up in the quaint little colliery town of Saunda. The youngest of four siblings, I had to learn my trades at an early age. But those golden moments and memories of friends, school, family, friendly neighbourhood dogs, and fruit-bearing trees still give me goosebumps. The kindest life fostered the spirit of compassion and empathy from the very beginning. Visiting ashrams and meeting yogis were some of the most inspiring moments of my life.

Childhood turned to adolescence. Passing out of school pushed me to the competitive world of would-be professionals. Shy by nature, it took me a while to muster the courage to speak to strangers. But friendship blossomed with the tiniest of droplets of love, kindness, and care. Even after many years I go down memory lane, and reminisce the simple life dotted with the small pleasures of street food, of hopping on the tram and spending leisurely time by the Ganges, of watching boats undulating on the sacred water of the Ganges.

Embarking on a Chef's Journey

When my course at college, the Institute of Hotel Management at Kolkata, came to an end, I took up my first assignment. It was with the first destination spa of India, Ananda in the Himalayas. Incidentally, I always found a resonance of army life in the

life of a chef. Learning fueled the passion, and the journey of spirituality seamlessly combined with the concept of a healthy lifestyle and food. Sitting by the River Ganges and listening to the chanting of mantras was my favourite relaxation time activity when I lived in Rishikesh. I could freely mingle with a mendicant, a sage, or a millionaire with the same ease. Rishikesh is the abode of God, it is said. And it was my abode for several years when the adult in me grew tired of the repetitive nature of barbs and opprobrium.

With a Michelin Star Chef

I was writing my parting letter to the organization I was working with even though I was apprehensive about my next assignment. The prospect of working for a Michelin Star chef was the next big thing for me. And this happened fortuitously. A journey that took me away from my homeland. The ultimate rendezvous with quality was never an easy one since I had a very humble beginning as a chef. It was an uphill task to be accepted by a kitchen dominated by Europeans, and I was the lone Indian waiting to blossom in the right environment. Devonshire, UK, beckoned.

The first assignment was to work with the ex-Ramsay's Chef Philip Phil, who was as temperamental as a protagonist, but the imprint that he left was indescribable. So many of the plates were banged, and so many of the things flew over my head during the service rush hours that it prompted me to learn my skill faster than others. I also learned about organic farming practices which influenced my life choices, and the decision to incorporate organic food in all my menus. The seed of the organic book that I came out with was engendered here.

Turning Author

It was never easy to decide to become a chef as I sauntered through my adolescence, for a larger part of it was rather due to a lack of viable options. No sooner did I discover a passion for cooking than I developed the knack of jotting down every relevant information to which my notebook bears testimony. The point is that this field is so replete with amazing information that even a thousand lives will fall short of chronicling all details and developments.

Upon returning from the UK, I took up a temporary assignment with the Hilton Shillim in the western ghats of India. It is at this place that I chronicled my tryst with organic food in the form of a book titled, *The Original Organic Cookbook*, that was published in the year 2008. In writing this book, or chronicling the progression of my career, was the desire to explore both the food as well as its potential beyond the confines of the kitchen, and also its aesthetic appeal to the gourmet and the common people.

An Assignment in Tanzania

Being inquisitive and experimental by nature, I decided to move to Tanzania in the year 2009. The Gibb's Farm Resort and Spa. Living with the Wambulu Masai tribe required some adjustment. The workplace resembled the bush kitchen with the traditional wood-fired oven, very old equipment, and a lot of love. The 100-acre farm was a literal treasure trove. Foraging at the farm was exciting as we kept finding unusual ingredients left behind by the previous gardener, and the still previous one, and so on. Every day was a lesson in art, culture, food, history, and tribal wisdom. The organic garden provided a perfect canvas for culinary expression. Soon awards followed, and the place created a niche for itself in the African continent for its sustainability, hospitality, and cuisine. Organic farming was a big part of what we did. The farm supplied us with more than 80% of our vegetable and fruit requirement. Besides, we also raised cattle, chickens, ducks, pigs, goats, and donkeys.

Back to India

Missing my homeland, I decided to move back to India, and work on a holistic retreat called Vana, at the foothills of Mussoorie. I got the opportunity to learn the art of living in the company of the masters and spiritual pursuers. I delved deeper to experience many other facets of life. Vana was the sanctuary of the senses, it was an abode for enhancing the quality of life. I had the privilege to serve His Holiness the Dalai Lama, and His

Holiness Sakya Trizin. Blessed by the masters, I soon embarked upon the journey to bring about awareness about organic food. As part of our commitment, we served the same quality of food to our team as we served to the guest. I also worked with the experts and agencies to help farmers turn to organic farming.

Off to Costa Rica

Little did I know that my next assignment would be in Latin America. Yes, after 6 wonderful years working with wonderful people and projects, I decided to work in another continent.

I embarked upon the journey to a small and beautiful country housing 5% of the global biodiversity. Costa Rica. My destination was the property called RISE, and the Kinkara Retreat Centre. On the second day of my arrival on the 800 acre farmland, I was mesmerized by the extent of advancement in agriculture. I learned permaculture principles. Permaculture is, amongst others, an approach to land management that adopts arrangements observed in flourishing natural ecosystems. It includes a set of design principles derived using whole systems thinking. It was a virtual paradise for everyone who lived in and around the place. Two brooks flowed within the property, providing plenty of water for the land. Here I got in touch with the Borucan tribes, and the custodians of the Mayan tradition. We explored the Mayan healing modes, and ended up planting more than 55 herbs, spices, shrubs, and medicinal plants which were part of the Mayan civilization before the conquistadors destroyed the culture. We trained the people from the neighbouring village to take up various roles available with the company. Conceived as a wellness community project, RISE was a futuristic project impacting the quality of life, education, food, community, and healing. It was a family-focused community that brought together residences, a Waldorf-inspired school, a certified organic farm, a fibre-connected co-working space, and a wellbeing retreat as a dynamic ecosystem. It has families that seek a life of creativity, joy, ease and prosperity.

This is where I started my next book project which hopefully should come out in the future. The book contains theories and practices for a healthy lifestyle, written especially for people wishing to connect with nature, and, therefore, to be able to make an informed choice about their life and living.

Sadly, the pandemic took a toll on this beautiful project, and brought about an end to my association with the land of "Pura Vida" - fun, frolic and wonder.

In The Maldives

In the year 2021 I took up an assignment to work on the first wellbeing island in the Maldives, a concept still in its nascent form. The sufferings from the pandemic motivated me to explore the world of immunity through food and lifestyle. My research will expand to include the study of nootropics, adaptogen, benefits of tea, ancient healing modes and beneficial substances, the food for happy hormones, and many other such aspects. The level of mindfulness affects us at both the gross and the subtle levels. This reflects in our day-to-day behavior, conduct, approach, energy level, and moods. I hope I will have some answers to alleviate the suffering of humans at the physical and psychological levels.

Change is the name of the game, and taking responsibility for your own life lies with you. It is easy once you make that special commitment to yourself. And once you make that sincere commitment to change, everything automatically starts to open, and improvement will come, and so very quickly, especially to an aware body and mind.

To draw from the Vedas:

May all sentient beings be at peace,
May no one suffer from illness,
May all see what is auspicious,
May none be distressed,
Om shanti shanti shanti.

❑❑❑

CHAPTER 4

The Many Genres of Designing and Illustrating

Suresh Kumar

As an illustrator and a designer, Suresh Kumar has designed and created art works in different genres. With a background in commercial art, he has worked in the area of advertising. He has illustrated for popular advertisements and comic strips, and developed characters for advertisements. He has designed advertising campaigns for a number of companies and NGOs. He has illustrated for various newspapers and books. He has also created a number of caricatures and cartoons. He has designed and sketched, with architects, layout plans, interiors and drawings of showrooms, exhibition halls and tableaux. He has also designed marriage and party sets as also

events for some companies. He has designed numerous postage stamps for India Post. Besides designing stamps, that makes for miniature art, he has also designed postal stationery and postmarks. He enjoys making oil, acrylic and water colour paintings, and has created a wide array of paintings. He also teaches art at college level. He is a wildlife enthusiast, and is also into wildlife photography.

As far as I can remember I used to draw. Maybe I have inherited it, as my uncles are good artists. While in first grade at school, my class teacher one day asked, "Is there anybody who can draw a peacock?" I raised my hand, and she gave me the chalk piece. I went to the blackboard, and drew a peacock, with the complete bloom, in the dancing posture. Everyone in the class exclaimed: "Wow!" And the teacher asked all the children to stand up and clap for me. From then on, I was known as, "The little artist"!

I did my first few years of schooling in Delhi where we were taught art. The last four years of my schooling were in the United Kingdom. There art is taken up seriously, and I did life drawings and pencil shadings, made oil colours and water colours. I had a good exposure there to serious art.

At the College of Art in Delhi

I got back to Delhi after finishing my schooling in 1982. I had science subjects, except for chemistry, at school in the UK. In Delhi to do a bachelor's in science or science-related subjects I had to have chemistry. So I was left with hardly any choice. Then somebody suggested the College of Art to me. I had never heard of this college before. The college was not particular on whether I had studied science or arts at senior school; I had to

have 60% and above marks at 12th grade. I had my marks in grades, and it worked out to 72%. And that was considered very good at the time. So I got into the College of Art.

The experience at college was awesome. We were exposed to the best in art, at the time, in and around Delhi. The number of students in the class being rather small, we were all quite close to each other. In my batch there were 60 students.

We all gained a great deal of experience. My college was situated near the Triveni Kala Sangam. There were artists who would come there, and would also come over to the college, and give talks. They would talk about their experience, how they trained, and also how they entered the art market. These were eye-openers for me. I had never thought of art as a serious pursuit, as a career. But these talks by artists revealed the opportunities and possibilities that art can offer.

At college, during the foundation course, all students had to do everything – sculpture, clay modelling, perspective drawing.

Specialization came in the second year of the course. Thirty of us in my batch were into commercial art. Commercial art is the stream where art knowledge is applied in commercial aspects. At that time commercial art was in demand in the advertising field. So commercial art revolved around the knowledge of design and art focused on advertising and marketing, and how to make a visual impact for a product to be sold.

During the third year of college itself, we got jobs from small time advertising agencies for doing cutting and pasting, and designing logos. Also, as the college was near Pragati Maidan, the large exhibition grounds, where the annual India International Trade Fair is also held, there were a lot of opportunities for us, students, there. We would go there, and design murals. I did many murals for the pavilions there such as those of Punjab, Kerala and Andhra Pradesh. Besides, there were private companies that were participating in the exhibitions, and had their stalls. Some of these stalls were designed and some of the art works were created by us, students. And we would be paid for the assignments.

Into the World of Advertising

After passing out of college I went into the advertising field, and worked for a couple of advertising agencies. In advertising agencies there would be a finishing artist who would do cutting and pasting, and some little odd jobs, and there would be specialists like illustrators, visualizers, art directors, and creative directors.

I was good at drawing and illustrating. In the place where I started working there was a lot of storyboards being created.

Storyboards refer to series of frames like a comic book where an advertising idea or a script is converted into frames. This helps a client understand what is being intended to shoot or visualize. I did a lot of storyboards. I figured out that my field is illustration. In the advertising field I was an illustrator. And illustration is what I pursued. A lot of my work has been published in the advertising field like the Hajmola cartoons, the Milky Bar kid cartoon strip, and illustrations for Nestle, the Milo, and McDonald's. I have done a lot of work over around 25 years illustrating for advertising agencies.

I am still into doing various kinds of illustrations where I use a lot of media like water colous, pencils, colour pencils, oil paints, acrylics, poster colours, and I also use software like Photoshop and CorelDraw.

An Interest in Philately

Over the years I have also been involved in postage stamp designing for the Indian postal department. It is interesting to go back to see how my association with this began and progressed. For kids in my time stamp collection was a very popular hobby. I was also one such kid interested in philately, and possessed many stamp collections. In fact, as a kid, I would, for fun, even cut out interesting pictures from colour magazines in the shape of postage stamps!

Back then, of course, as a youngster, I never knew there is a career based on stamp designing. Later when I was in the final year of college, the fourth year, I, along with a couple of other students, got selected from the college to attend a stamp designers' camp in Nasik. It was a 2-week long program that had students from art colleges across India. As part of this we would be given a subject, and asked to design stamps.

We were around 30 or 35 students, and it was a very good experience as we were right there in the press, at Nasik, that prints India's postage stamps. The press had some senior artists, and they would tell us the do's and don'ts associated with stamp designing. Since we were in the press we were exposed to the limitations, and the security aspects, and everything concerning designing and producing a postage stamp.

Experts from the field of philately would also come, and we would have two-hour long interactions with them where they would share their experience with us, and give us advice on these matters. One such person who came there was Mr Sharma, the director (philately) of the postal department from Delhi. He invited the three of us who were from Delhi, to go over and meet him at his office at the department of post. And that is what we did. He suggested that since we were almost passing out of college, he would give us some work. We were commissioned to design postage stamps on the topic of alternative energy specifically solar energy. Unfortunately, my design did not get approved. But the postal department would call me thereafter to design some material. That was it then, and the association came to an end because I was into advertising, and there was a lot of work in it. And there was hardly any time to do any work for the postal department.

Subsequently I was also working for a number of publications as a freelancer. One of the magazines was Target, which was specifically for children. I was doing a lot of comic strips for the magazine. It was a collaborative work: I would draw the comics, and the dialogues would be written by a writer. One of the writers there, Swapna Dutta, who found my drawings to be good, suggested I go over and meet her husband who was then the director (philately) in the postal department. So I went and met him, and told him of the work experience I had. He assigned me a stamp designing job. And the design I created actually made it to the stamp issued by the postal department. Having done my first stamp, I was empanelled on the department's list of artists. That is when my serious work in designing postage stamps for India's postal department started.

Designing Postage Stamps

Designing stamps is interesting work. Research work would be required on the theme of a stamp for which one is commissioned. For this one may have to visit libraries, museums, and offices, and look up books, photographs and other material concerning the subject.

The art work for the design of a stamp should suit and reflect the theme of the stamp. I, of course, prefer line illustrations for the stamp designs I come up with. With line illustrations clarity is ensured because stamps are ultimately brought out in small sizes.

As regards dimensions of the stamp to be designed this is given to the designer, and is according to the sizes available at the press. This is based on the parameter of perforations. Stamps are issued in rectangular and square shapes, and also in unique shapes such as triangular, circular and hexagonal.

Over the years, since 1994, I have designed numerous commemorative stamps for India Post. The stamps, issued on diverse themes, in the form of se-tenants or single stamps, have depicted various aspects of India as also international issues and events. The stamps have portrayed renowned personalities, significant institutions, and important occasions. The stamps on the theme of fashion, for instance, that I designed were issued in a series, containing a total of 21 stamps.

Besides postage stamps, I have designed first day covers (FDCs) and brochures, and also a few cancellations (postmarks), as also some special postal covers.

Illustrating and Beyond

In art, which is my passion and profession, illustration is my main area of work. Besides stamp designing, I am into doing illustrations for advertising agencies and NGOs (non-governmental organizations). I am also into teaching. I have been teaching at various colleges. I also teach youngsters who are going to take entrance exams at art institutions. I also teach a group of women keenly interested in learning the basic techniques of drawing and painting. Teaching is something I really enjoy because, at this point in time, there is indeed a lot of experience I have, and am more than willing to share.

Besides art, I am also a wildlife enthusiast. I love to travel, and to explore places especially within India such as the remote North-East. And now I would love to visit Kashmir. I enjoy going to places of historical importance and to wildlife areas. I am also into wildlife photography. I am part of a group of wildlife enthusiasts, and we go to various national parks. Close to Delhi is the Jim Corbett National Park which I have visited some seven or eight times. I would like to visit national parks all across India.

When I look at the larger picture what seems to be motivational and inspirational is the glorious civilizational history of India. For instance, our contribution to the wellness of the world. Likewise, the many spiritual masters in our country. And we can connect with a master of our choice. I get motivated by the great spiritual masters. While working, most of the time I listen in to the masters' talks. Along with some inspirational music which goes well with that. Currently I listen to Sri M and Sadhguru. We have answers to our questions in life right within us. We just need to get reconnected with our own selves. This is a motivation in itself. And this should motivate not just the youth, but everyone.

❑❑❑

CHAPTER 5

Spiritual Calling – Thy Name is Faith and Patience

Dr Sweta C Saxena

With a bachelor's degree in economics from the Lady Shri Ram College for Women, Delhi University, a master's degree in economics from the Delhi School of Economics, and a doctorate degree in economics from the University of Washington, USA, Dr Sweta C Saxena is an economist who has worked on economic issues around the world. She began her career as an assistant professor at the University of Pittsburgh, USA. This was followed by a stint at the Bank for International Settlements in Basel, Switzerland. Subsequently she worked at the International Monetary Fund in USA. In her next assignment she worked as Chief in the macroeconomic policy and financing for development

division at the UN Economic and Social Commission for Asia and the Pacific (UNESCAP) in Bangkok, Thailand. She is currently Chief of Staff at the United Nations Economic Commission for Africa (UNECA) in Addis Ababa, Ethiopia. She is a widely published economist. She has also written occasionally on Buddhist economics. She is also deeply into the reading of the Vedas and the Gita. She is a travel buff, and has travelled world over. But all the same she enjoys cooking paranthas and khadi at home, and proudly dons Indian attires, with the bindi in place.

By now, I have lived more than half of my life outside of India. While I visit Delhi often, and am always in touch with my family and friends, it is hard to find in what life in Delhi now is any sort of semblance to the life I lived when I was growing up in the city. So much has changed.

Schooling in Delhi

Yes, I grew up in an era where we had few materials things but many people that gave wonderful memories. I grew up in a large family with five siblings, and, at some points in time, numerous cousins. We lived a modest life, and if it was not for the sacrifice of my parents, we would have never been able to attend private schools. But being able to pay the school fees was one thing and to maintain the living standards like that of my friends was another. We could not afford to travel, hence I spent all my summer vacations at home, playing with my cousins. I recall that on return to school after the summer, we were often asked to write an essay on: How I spent my summer vacation. Since the teacher would never be impressed with a write-up on spending time with cousins, I used to write

fictional stories of places. For the autumn break, I would spend all the ten days with my cousins at my grandmother's place in the walled city area (Old Delhi), and watch the enactment of Lord Ram's life (Ram Lila), and the burning of the effigy of Ravana (signifying the victory of good over evil). I must admit that I still hold all those memories with my cousins too close to my heart, and would never trade it for anything in the world. Additionally, I have never held a grudge against my parents or God about not giving us the means to travel like my friends.

Yes, family expectations from us were different, and we respected elders, even when we disagreed on some issues. In high school, we did not have much choice, but to go with the family's decisions and societal pressures. Being a good student

puts one on the list of to-be-doctors/engineers. Accordingly, I was a pure science student, studying physics, chemistry, biology and mathematics. After the first day in the biology lab, where I jumped more than the rat that I was to dissect, I knew I did not want to be and/or could not be a doctor. I was not allowed to move to the science with economics stream. And so I continued with the subjects in the science stream I was in.

Pursuing Higher Education

What after school? What do you do with a bachelor's degree in mathematics or chemistry or even physics? There were not many opportunities. Of course, I was also a very good writer, but majoring in English was not a career choice my family wanted to leave me with. How would one make a living with a degree in English literature? Of course, Jhumpa Lahiri and JK Rowling were not around to give a concerned parent some hope that their own child may be able to make a decent living. As my well-wishers my parents had my best interest in mind.

Fate had strange things up its sleeve. While I respected my family's decision to opt for the science stream in school, they respected mine in college to take up economics (always remember, respect is a two-way street!). They only forewarned me that it was a very difficult stream, and since I did not want them to have the opportunity to say, "We told you so" if I failed, I worked hard. After graduating from the Lady Shri Ram College for Women, Delhi, I wanted to do a master's in economics from the Delhi School of Economics. This was as far as my ambitions ran.

Off to USA for Further Studies and Research

We were living in a time when there were no jobs even after graduating from premier institutions. Hence, I decided to do a PhD. I spent the next year taking the Graduate Record Examination, the GRE for short, and filling out applications so I could pursue my PhD in the United States. No matter where I would get admission, I just knew that I could only go if I got full scholarship. Lo and behold, I received the kind of offer I could not refuse, and I made my way to the other side of the world and landed in Seattle.

Life took me on a path I had never imagined. I studied hard in graduate school, and was at the top of my class. After 4 years, I joined my first job as an assistant professor in the Public Policy School at the University of Pittsburgh. It was great to teach masters and PhD level students, and oversee their theses, while doing my own independent academic research. That research took me to many international conferences in Korea, Japan and New Zealand, and other places.

Work has Taken me Places

I then got an opportunity to work at the Bank for International Settlements in Basel, Switzerland. Living and working in Switzerland changed me in more fundamental ways than I had asked for. The country and its people had their own peculiar ways of living, and one had to get used to it to be able to survive. This led me to practise mindfulness, and I concentrated on changing myself rather than changing those two million Swiss. Living in Switzerland gave me the opportunity to travel all over Europe, before I made a return to the United States, this time at the International Monetary Fund in Washington DC. I started in the African Department and worked on fragile countries (Sierra Leone and South Sudan). This got me visiting those countries, and meeting their people.

Destiny brought me full circle, closer to home. I would not say that hopping from one institution to another was my hobby. Rather, since 2013, I have been contemplating how my professional life as an economist is in line with our tradition of mindful living. This led me to write a blog that questioned the assumptions made in economics regarding our methods of production and consumption, and it also related how technology alters our behaviors. I began contemplating on all this in 2013, and it appears there were others too thinking along those lines.

Towards a Beginning in Changing the Narrative in Economics

In 2018 I got an opportunity to lead the flagship publication at the Asia-Pacific arm for the United Nation located in Bangkok. I knew right away that this would be a great move towards changing the narrative in economics away from the short-term focus on economic growth towards longer term issues like inequality and climate change. It helped me work on topics dear to my heart – ensuring that no individual or country is left behind; that our production and consumption patterns respect planetary boundaries; and that we are resilient to any shock, economic or non-economic. In this regard, I built my own personal resilience during the pandemic as I steeped myself in Vedic literature. It gave me a perspective on our existence, and what constitutes a good life. Since then, I am reading the Bhagavad Gita and the Srimad Bhagavatam for my daily dose of religiosity and spirituality.

Needless to say, the move to Bangkok not only brought me closer to home (India – physically, culturally, and spiritually) but being in the center of Asia, gave me umpteen opportunities to travel in the region. Thanks to all the work I did to change this narrative, I became a member of an OECD (Organization for Economic Co-operation and Development) network that wants to promote the new thinking on adapting to the new challenges of our times. Also, in 2021 the Government Economists for New Economic Systems (GENESYS) was launched as a platform for debating, experimenting and discussing policy alternatives and the analytical approaches which underpin them.

Meanwhile, God had more plans for me to make a mark. As I ended my tenure at the UNESCAP in Bangkok, I was offered to be the chief of staff at the United Nations Economic Commission for Africa (UNECA) in Addis Ababa, Ethiopia. This is a region very close to my heart as I started my career at the IMF in the African Department. As the chief of staff, I am expected to help push boundaries on the policy front, and help the region jump start on its development path. I am very excited to be in Addis Ababa, and look forward to the challenges in this new assignment.

Seeing the Bigger Plans

In a nutshell, God has been kind. In a life full of twists and turns, along the way I learned that I was not given the opportunity to travel as a kid so that I would learn to value relationships with people – my family, and extended family. When I was sent to a foreign country (Switzerland) where my material life improved multifold, I was made to feel terrible so I could search for spirituality. When I felt that the world was going topsy-turvy, and I was working at an institution that did not help make things better, I was given an opportunity to work at a place where I could make a difference. And then when I look back at those school days when I did not travel like my classmates, I find that I eventually visited every place that I learned of in my geography class – trekking through Patagonia; safaris in the Savannah, drive through the rift valley; climbing Mt. Kilimanjaro; watching iguanas in the Galapagos; celebrating the Carnival in Rio de Janeiro; being at the top of the Great Wall of China. All it required was a little patience, and a lot of faith in God.

❑❑❑

CHAPTER 6

Sowing the SEEDS of Change

Dr Manu Gupta

It was when they were pursuing their studies at the School of Planning and Architecture (SPA), New Delhi, that a few students set up the Sustainable Environment and Ecological Development Society (SEEDS) in the year 1993. One of the co-founders of SEEDS is Dr Manu Gupta, who continued to be actively involved in the NGO. After a bachelor's in planning (BPlan) and a master's in planning (MPlan) from the SPA, he went on to do his PhD in community-based disaster management from the Kyoto University, Japan.

SEEDS is into creating community resilience through practical solutions in the areas of disaster readiness, response and rehabilitation. Dr Manu Gupta has passionately and relentlessly worked in the area of disaster management. He is currently the vice president of SEEDS. He is on the boards of several regional and global organizations such as the Asian Disaster Reduction and Response Network (ADRRN). He is now working towards widening the ambit of his community-owned disaster management approach from Asia-Pacific to around the globe. He has been elected an Ashoka Fellow. He is part of various national committees of the government of India. He is also a visiting faculty to several global institutions.

For the past two-and-one-half decades, I have been involved in the work of helping people affected by disasters. In the year 1998 the cyclone that hit the coast of Gujarat in Kandla took away more than 3000 precious human lives in just a few hours. Even though it was not a severe cyclone, the systems failure was apparent. Thousands of poor workers working in the salt pans in the Rann of Kutch lost their lives because they did not get any warning in time. Many were fatally injured because the thin tin roofs of their homes hit them even as they flew like missiles.

A few years earlier, in the canteen of Delhi's School of Planning and Architecture, a few kindred spirits had come together to form the Sustainable Environment and Ecological Development Society (SEEDS), a non-profit organisation. Anshu and I were among the co-founders who decided to continue the journey beyond college. With just our *curious passion* driving us, much of our initial years was spent in exploration and learning.

As soon as we heard about the Kandla cyclone, we hopped on to a train to go to the cyclone affected area ready to volunteer as relief workers. Volunteering to offer aid after the Kandla

cyclone was our first direct experience of working in an area devastated by a disaster. The destroyed homes, uprooted trees, tall electric poles bent to the ground, and, worst of all, the trauma in peoples' eyes shook us to the core.

Finding My Mission

Our experience in the Kandla cyclone followed by that in an earthquake in the Himalayas and then a devastating cyclone in Odisha, and we were sure what we wanted to do. It was an inner call. We felt that as professionals with access to the best of knowledge, we owe it to society to use the knowledge where it is truly needed. Building capacity of the most vulnerable communities to prevent and prepare for disasters became our mission. Our initial experiences convinced us that it is possible. There is enough knowledge and technology in place that can, for example, help build earthquake-resistant houses at minimal costs. And, likewise, there is technology that is available to ensure advance weather warning that can reach everyone. Organisations like SEEDS could play the role of 'bridging' the knowledge and practice gap.

We have since worked with over 3 million people across India and neighbouring countries, and had 'boots on the ground' in over 35 major emergencies.

We co-created and replicated new models of collaboration with affected communities, enabling them to be more resilient to future shocks and stresses.

The Learning Curve

The first decade of my professional career was primarily field-based learning. In the process, I seem to have unlearnt a lot of my formal education. The fact that people who struggle to survive in disasters eventually find ways to adapt, and still find happiness provides an exciting opportunity to harness a latent potential. I took this as the premise for a doctoral study, to test models of community-led disaster management practices where the role of external assistance agencies could just be of support.

The ensuing model of community-led practice recognizes at the 'heart' that every human being, irrespective of their circumstances, has a right to dignity, well-being and control over her/his own life. The model has now led to many new pathways of practice applied to different situations of disaster response, rehabilitation and readiness for future disasters.

After the devastating earthquake in Gujarat in 2001, we decided to stay back in a village – Patanka, and carry out

reconstruction work along with the people. The two years spent with the community was a great learning experience. Understanding their challenges, and going back to the drawing board every evening to creatively look for best answers helped in moving forward one step at a time. Building mutual trust achieved through actions on the ground, demonstrating what works through one's own actions on the ground, was key in creating models of collaboration that have been long lasting. By the end of the intervention, the people in Patanka felt empowered, and ready to face any disaster in future without having to suffer any loss. In return, I learnt, from them, how we can work in partnerships - away from 'project cycle' mind-sets by understanding priorities, and local limitations; and thinking out-of-the-box to embrace unexplored opportunities.

The Patanka experience, and many subsequent ones, reinforced our confidence in the collaboration model which we have replicated widely, and advocated to governments and international agencies for creating enabling policy environments.

Influencing Systems Change

Word of our experiments spread across borders. Chance meetings in conferences, and papers written in international publications helped connect with people from other parts of the world as also with the United Nations. These connections soon developed into strong bonds of friendship that led to joint advocacy efforts and solidarity, initially at Asia level, and subsequently with Africa and the rest of the world.

I am now on the boards of several international organisations where we jointly pursue the goals of stronger decentralisation and empowerment of the people. Today it gives me immense satisfaction to see that many of the advocacy efforts at international forums have created global policy shifts.

In the context of making a shift from policy to enabling practices, one of the many interesting initiatives of SEEDS is of working on the concept of 'transition shelters' as opposed to building temporary shelters in disaster-hit areas. Transition shelters are built keeping in mind the long-term recovery needs of affected communities. These structures have strong foundations built from locally sourced materials, are inexpensive, and quick to make. SEEDS has demonstrated this through transition shelters built in 14 emergencies across very different geographies and cultures. The successfully tried concept of transition shelters has drastically changed the rehabilitation and recovery process in India. The government of India has recognized this as a critical step in the recovery and reconstruction phase of a disaster, and introduced it in the national policy guidelines. Internationally too this practice has become a new norm encouraging humanitarian agencies, providing homes to those who have lost them to disasters, to think long-term, and allow a dignified transition from the immediate.

Inspiration

What has shaped me as a person the most is an early encounter with Buddhist philosophy that led to belief in my own inherent potential, and the ability to see the same in others. This has helped me never give up on people even when there were moments in my professional career when complete collapse was imminent. And likewise to remain humble and focused when we received top accolades from governments and international agencies. Developing the capacity to stand alone, believing in myself, and sometimes a friendly nudge from colleagues and family has kept me going. Inspiration from my mentor, and motivational words by the world's great leaders have brought hope in the darkest of times. As for instance this particular one from Rev. Martin Luther King Jr.: "If you can't fly then run, if you can't run then walk, if you can't walk then crawl, but whatever you do you have to keep moving forward."

The Future

Somewhere, I did realise that many of the initiatives require more than a lifetime to take shape. Perhaps, sub-consciously, constant efforts and new initiatives, and new friends, have also led to new institutions being built. Looking back, I feel at least some of these institutions have the ability to outlive me. I have been on founding boards of several international, national and local civil society alliances and associations. For getting people together for a common good. For me it has been about building resilience of disaster-affected people. It has helped me sow seeds for a shared value and legacy we can leave behind in the world.

At the same time, working with young people – encouraging them to take the lead, allowing them to make mistakes – has helped create a cadre that can take over soon. I am fortunate that I have such young friends all over the world from different nationalities and ethnicities with whom I share a deep bond of friendship and camaraderie.

This decade, 2020-30, is the 'make-it or break-it' decade for humanity. I am pinning my hopes on these youthful successors, who can take on the growing scale and complexity of the global challenges of disasters made much worse thanks to climate change. As SEEDS, we hope we will be able to transition successfully from being an explorer, to a learner, to a provider, and finally to an enabler institution without losing sight of our core founding spirit - our boots remaining firmly on the ground, and our spirit of *curious passion* never dying.

❑❑❑

CHAPTER 7

Travel Musings of a Wanderlust

Dr Rajani Rao

After completing her graduation in statistics in 1994, she did an MBA in Finance, followed by a stint in the IT sector. She also ran an eco-tourism enterprise. Thereafter she did a master's program in philosophy, and followed it up with a PhD in environmental philosophy from Mysore University. Dr Rajani Rao thus combined the study of environment and philosophy. A nature lover and keen environmentalist, she has facilitated the conducting of nature camps and activities on environment at the Indian Institute for Adventure Applications, Shimoga, Karnataka. She is a co-founder and member of Prakruthi Foundation, an NGO set up in 2008 to support the education needs of tribal/village schools and colleges. Passionate about travel, she has done various bike expeditions and other travels in India, and has undertaken journeys panning

five continents. Her interest in travel led to a curiosity to learn about environmental teachings from Indian philosophy, and its relevance in present times. She has authored 3 books under the title The Travails of a Pillion Rider as Cultural Diaries, Coastal Diaries and Camping Diaries. She conducts workshops on globetrotting skills in Bengaluru. She seeks to infuse the passion of sustainable travelling in women and the youth in colleges.

A skill is the ability to engage in a particular activity or do a particular work expertly. Globetrotting is one such skill that is a prerequisite for the current generation. It is the need of the hour as the world has become a global village where travel to any place is just a click away. The simple meaning of globetrotting is the act of travelling around the global sphere. In today's world there is truth in the age-old saying: A journey of a thousand miles begins with a single step. And this definitely propels one to become a globetrotter. A globetrotter is a person who travels widely. I would like to share some of the learnings which influenced me, and widened my knowledge during my globetrotting spree.

Adventure Gone Awry in Forest Terrain

It was an encounter with an elephant in the year 2012 that left an everlasting imprint in my memory. At the end of a week-long trip traversing the interiors of Karnataka by bike as a pillion, we – my friend Balaganesh (Bali) who was riding the bike and I – reached Kyathadevara Gudi or KG forest reserve in Chamarajanagar district to spend New Year's Eve with friends. They had come directly from Bengaluru. The next morning, our friends in two cars, and ourselves on the bike, were riding towards the Biligiriranga temple located in the forest premises when we were suddenly charged upon by a lone tusker. Bali, who was riding the bike, suffered serious injuries. I had small bruises on the right knee, but nothing major. The elephant tried to push Bali off the bike by puncturing his abdomen, twisting his left leg, crushing his feet, and half-tearing his thighs. In the process Bali fell on his side, and fractured his right shoulder. It was a nightmarish situation, but with the collective efforts of our friends, we rushed him to a hospital at Mysuru. The doctors attending on him opined that he would need a minimum of two years to recover completely. But to everyone's joy, he was back on his feet, travelling and riding his bike, in six months flat. The fast recovery can solely be attributed to his following a regular physical fitness regime, and possessing a phenomenal mental strength to stay rooted through life's uncertainties. His enduring the pain, resilience to overcome the setbacks, and positive outlook is a survival lesson in itself. The deepest learning for me was to not take perfect health for granted, but work towards having a healthy lifestyle. This episode would have deterred one from further travels, but Bali continued his expeditions to go to Kenya, do scuba diving in Lakshadweep, and many more such adventure activities. Indeed, one should never fear stepping out, as most fears arise out of imagination, and in reality do not materialize. I understood that having an affirmative mindset helps to overcome any unfortunate incident one might end up facing in travel or in life.

A Bike Trip to Ladakh

My first long expedition as a pillion biker was to Ladakh in the year 2016. It took 33 days to do the return trip from Bengaluru to

Ladakh covering a distance of around 8,000 kms. Out of many learnings, the one that has remained on my mind is to enjoy the journey even while aiming for the goal. It is not always about reaching the destination, but to savour the learnings from the ups and downs of the path trodden.

Having reached Leh the previous day, 7 friends in 3 Royal Enfield bikes and a Mahindra Thar vehicle set out towards Pangong Tso, which is the highest brackish water lake in the world. It is one of the main tourist attractions, apart from the Khardung La pass that I was dreaming of visiting. It had become hugely popular thanks to the Hindi movie 3 Idiots. Motoring the incredible heights and winding passes in these mountainous regions is a lifetime experience.

We left in the morning, and after riding a certain distance detoured onto a makeshift mud road which was filled with loose gravel. While negotiating a steep curve, our bike's clutch plate gave way. We had to make a quick decision, be decisive, and communicate the same to others. The only option was to return to Leh. We were not hugely disappointed as such unforeseen things do happen. It is part and parcel of a traveller's journey. Our friends continued ahead as we dissuaded them from coming along with us. We met them the next day at another location after getting the bike repaired. Going with the flow, and adapting to changing situations will sometimes throw pleasant surprises too. Like in this case. For in Leh the evening time was spent in visiting a few unexplored places, and plus we got to ride through Khardung La pass twice over - onwards and back.

On Bike along 'Bharat Mala'

The above expedition, and several week-long tours, pillion riding on bike, helped me be ready and fit for a unique travel idea conjured by Bali, my co-traveller. It was his 18 year-long cherished dream to shoot the sunset and sunrise photos, and time-lapse videos at the Indian beaches. In 2018 I had the opportunity to accompany him from Lakhpat in Gujarat to Gosaba in West Bengal. Along India's coast, nicknamed 'Bharat Mala' – the necklace of India, I was a pillion rider for 52 days covering 11,600 kms by bike. Since the journey covered 9 states and 2 union territories, the major part was to draw up a tentative route map touching the coastal beaches. We kept a comfortable ride of 150 – 200 odd kms to hop from one beach to another. Accordingly, the stay options at specific locations suiting our budget were noted. This also was a testing time to be minimalistic in carrying items like clothes, camera and bike accessories. It is a myth that we need more. The journey was a breeze with less luggage; it was tension-free. Only the most essential things got packed as everything had to fit in the two

saddle bags strung on the side of the bike. The entire gamut of planning, logistics and budgeting was done in advance. This came in handy, and helped in easy navigation on the actual expedition. However, the pre-planned night halts at a few places had to be changed because of non-availability of staying options near the beaches. Having a plan helps, but one should not be rigid, and, if need be, tweak them wherever required. We should be part of a solution, and not the problem. Travelling at a stretch for two months gave me an opportunity to interact with locals everywhere, and to spread the awareness related to: 'not to misuse plastic'.

Exploring Emperor Ashoka's Edicts

Subsequently, in 2019 I wanted to explore Emperor Ashoka's rock and pillar edicts that are located at several places in Karnataka. This time I was a co-passenger in a four-wheeler. Emperor Ashoka was a lover of nature, and implemented various measures to safeguard the environment. His rock and pillar inscriptions are protected monuments now under the care of the Archeological Survey of India (ASI). The journey took us to interior places like Sanatti, Maski, Nittur, Udegolam, and Gavimath that were near the towns of Kalaburagi, Raichur, Bellary, and Koppal respectively. It was interesting to note the choice of specific rock locations used for inscriptions. I wondered how often people could, in those days, have accessed them to read the proclamations, as quite a few were located up on hilltops. Most of the residents whom we met during our trip knew about their existence, but had no in-depth knowledge of its importance. King Ashoka's edicts spread Buddha's teachings for the benefit of future generations - to take care of the environment, be kind to elders, and perform good deeds. This expedition had its own charm as it was not a normal trip. We went in search of these rock edicts with a bare minimum knowledge about their whereabouts. Google maps failed to locate a couple of them, suggesting that one cannot be over-dependent on technology. Such an offbeat journey still mandated the good old way of asking locals for directions. A strong reminder that not everything is geo-tagged. My huge learning was with respect to managing time efficiently - to cover 8 places spread out wide in 3 short days. Due to the remoteness and inaccessibility of these locations, I could not physically see three of them. An equally important aspect learnt was to prioritize, and forego if it is not feasible to see everything on the list. Some things have to be set aside to be enjoyed some other time. Each visit, if only to the same place, in truth, feels different because of the difference in seasons, the changing times, and our own altering reflections.

Travelling to discover the Environment – Philosophy Connect

Travelling was an integral part of my growing up because of my father's transferable bank job. The umpteen travels I had with my family played an important role in infusing me with the passion to explore, thus making me a globetrotter. As a traveller, I chanced upon learning from the various journeys which manifested in doing a doctorate in environment philosophy. I could see a closer connection between travel and nature which helped me grow as a person. There were Vedic verses which caught my attention while studying my masters in philosophy that have had a profound effect on me, and truly influenced my thoughts. Here are some of them:

> *Proper utilization of the elements (ether, air, water, fire, earth) helps in spreading health and happiness.*
>
> **– (Yajur Veda 1.2.25, 27/1.1.28/1.3.16, 19/1.4.2, 31/1.6.10/1.13.42)**

> *O Air, you are our father, our protector.*
>
> **– (Rig Veda 10.186.2)**

> *Oceans are treasures of wealth and hence need protection.*
>
> **– (Yajur Veda 38.22)**

The Sun's rays are powerful enough to drive away not only man's physical diseases, but also his evil ideas.

– (Rig Veda 5.29.10, 7.76.1, 7.45.3, 6.52.6)

Earth is a paradise for man and all beings, as it has the sanction of nature's reward.

– (Atharvana Veda 5.30.6)

Travel brings out the vagaries of different things that one cannot assume, but can always be felt. The many years of travelling has made me introspect deep within, to experience the newness of each day, and cherish the unfolding mystery. I enjoy being in tune with nature from whence we get all our inspiration. It has aided me to be more mindful, lead a minimalist life, show gratitude, and be humble. It has helped me share some of these travels through writing the book titled, *The Travails of a Pillion Rider* which has three Diaries (three books in the Travails series): *Cultural Diaries*, *Coastal Diaries* and *Camping Diaries*.

One should always be eager to explore, and be ever ready to learn which makes travel blissful. These globetrotting skills learnt one step at a time make a huge impact not only in our travels, but in our daily living too.

Travel, as it makes one wiser!

❑❑❑

CHAPTER 8

In the Quest for Organicity, Sustainability and Balance

Ananthoo

Ananthasayanan, popularly known as Ananthoo, was doing a stint of his career, as a telecom and IT professional, in Switzerland when he decided to move back to India in 2006. He co-founded Tula to create the Tula line of organic clothing. He is based in Chennai, and has been working towards promoting the organic way of food and clothing. He is associated with the Safe Food Alliance, Alliance for Sustainable and Holistic Agriculture, India HandMade Collective, and Non-Violent Economy Network. He has also worked in the Millets Mission of the Tamil Nadu State Planning Commission.

I am (was?) a telecom engineer by profession, and worked in the telecom and IT sector. The last stint of six years of my professional career was in Switzerland. Ever since I came back to India in 2006, I have not been in any monetarily gainful employment. I work only for social causes, predominantly in the areas of safe food, sustainable agriculture, rural livelihoods and cotton value chain.

As one of the co-founders of Tula I am deeply involved in the enterprise. I am also a coordinator with the Safe Food Alliance which seeks to promote safe and organic food; secure nourishing food for all; and grow food that makes soil fertile, restores the environment and secures farmers' livelihoods. I am also associated with the Alliance for Sustainable and Holistic Agriculture, ASHA, a national network of farmer organisations, unions, NGOs and activists, working on sustainable agriculture and farmers' livelihoods. I coordinate and convene the market-related activities towards setting up a market for organic produce from small farmers across the nation.

I have also worked closely with the Tamil Nadu State Planning Commission in the Millets Mission to promote millets to combat malnutrition, and also help farmers overcome drought and climate change crises.

Setting up Tula

I would like to share with you the journey of Tula. In Sanskrit Tula (pronounced *toola*) means cotton. It also means balance or equilibrium (pronounced *tulaa*). Tula is an enterprise combining both restoring an equilibrium in cotton value chain. A not-for-profit social enterprise, it creates garments from

traditional Indian desi cotton grown by smallholder farmers on rainfed farms. The yarn is hand spun by skilled khadi workers, and coloured with natural dyes, with expert guidance, where required. The fabric is woven on handlooms by master weavers, and the garments stitched by women and men from economically and socially marginalised groups. Tula garments are perhaps the lightest garments possible, both in terms of the environmental impact and its fair trade sense, and also the most eco-friendly ones. Tula works to revive and encourage the rich artisanal traditions of India.

At a time when our Indian farmers and artisans were in dire need of support, we, fifteen like-minded friends, decided to step in, and make a difference by bringing a niche clothing line to revive rainfed desi cotton, making sure everyone involved gets remunerated well enough to rise above their merely subsistence levels.

Each of us, fifteen friends, invested Rs one lakh, so that with Rs fifteen lakhs we commenced the initiative. A few among us are involved actively to date. It is with humility and pride that one can say that Tula returned the sum to the respective investors in five years of operation.

Since its inception, in 2014, up until now, only the initial investment has been re-invested time and again leading to gross sales of over Rs fifty lakhs each year since 2015. The Tula business runs very efficiently by itself without having the need for outside resources, operating as a viable not-for profit enterprise, and striving to touch more livelihoods with the same investment. Tula has managed to touch and empower some three hundred livelihoods directly. Though we set out to operate only in Tamil Nadu, Tula expanded to Karnataka and Maharashtra with the same investment, and thus tripled its operation and net with the same money through financial discipline.

From Organic Food to Organic Fibre

Tula has its roots in our efforts and experience with organic farming of indigenous foods. The movement began in 2007 in Chennai when we, the group of friends including me, got together to address the grave issue of farmer suicides ravaging India. Also, the poison on our plates, by way of the chemicals that are a part of agricultural produce, and the eventual health and environmental crises this would lead to, was a big concern. Thus was born the non-profit, volunteer-run organic store in Chennai, reStore, working closely with farmers and consumers to increase both the demand and supply of local food as well as create awareness about safe food. On one side reStore helped farmers move to sustainable agriculture using traditional agricultural methods, and on the other a fair market was created for the organic produce grown. Subsequently, through a collective and community approach, the Organic Farmers Market (OFM) came about. It built a strong network, with many youngsters and volunteers joining the movement, taking organic, safe food to customers across Chennai through a network of stores. The twice-a-week veggie bazaars became a special attraction. Not only was a bigger demand and greater awareness for safe organic food created, but also farmers' produce got marketed more. Both reStore and OFM ensured traceability and transparency; organicity; and fair price to both farmers and consumers. Priority was given to small and marginal farmers, and efforts were made to popularise and restore traditional food like millets, traditional rice varieties and healthy snacks. Last year, for instance, OFM brought to the fore 81 traditional rice varieties—white, brown, red and black.

In 2013, we, the group of friends, sat down to evaluate the success of our efforts. There were questions about the continuing farm suicides, and on whether our efforts were as successful as we thought. There was the issue of a high percentage of farm suicides in the cotton belt. Also there was the invasion of genetically modified (GM) cotton, BT (Bacillus thuringiensis) cotton. It was a matter of concern that farmers had to buy these expensive seeds season after season, and not

save seeds by themselves, the way it had been hitherto since ten thousand years. The pesticide consumption for the BT cotton crops was also enormous unlike what was touted. There was also an unavailability of native seeds for farmers to use. There were thus more issues than we could envisage, and tougher problems to address than we thought with respect to cotton. It was not like food that only entailed growing the crop sustainably; trying to revive sustainable practices; and restore nature, health and livelihoods. With cotton it was more complicated and complex.

The Tula Approach: Tackling the Cotton Value Chain

Cotton was a different ball game. None of us had a clue about the cotton value chain. We wanted to take the harvested organic cotton through to the end—from farm to garments—*Khet se kapda tak*. But what would be the steps involved? We set off to travel to the cotton belt to see what was happening, documenting the value chain.

Going back in time, khadi had been a symbol of our freedom struggle, propagated and supported by Mahatma Gandhi, and later by Vinoba Bhave and J C Kumarappa. Cotton and khadi played a large, symbolic role in signifying sovereignty and self-rule. Khadi was about a life style, the local economy, rural livelihoods and ecological sustainability. In the year 1947 desi cotton varieties—short to medium staple—were grown on about 92% area of the country's cotton growing belt, and the foreign long staple on just around 8%. Desi cotton was always accompanied by manual spinning and hand weaving of the most skilled and aesthetic kind making India world-famous for its textiles.

But now what we got to see on the ground was shocking. The industrial processing and the high-energy, high-investment mills had displaced thousands of rural artisans, and the massive pollution and ecological damage it was creating, for instance, by way of chemical dyeing, was unsustainable and hazardous. Add to that the exploitation and poor working conditions of workers. The handloom sector had been the second largest employer after farming. What had happened to our traditional seeds? To our artisans? To our practices? At every point, from farm to fibre, it was heart-wrenching. Cotton and khadi were in serious crisis. Incidentally, our Indian flag too was being made from BT cotton. What became of the lofty ideal of self-reliance linked to khadi? Also, the compensation offered for the various jobs like hand spinning, hand weaving, and tailoring was measly. Wherever we travelled the scene was bleak and horrific. It was not just about BT cotton versus desi seeds and organic cotton, but rather the whole value chain – spinning, weaving, dyeing and tailoring – that had to be worked upon.

We decided we would (re)imagine a highly ethical, eco-friendly value chain. The Tula experiment set off by having 15 dryland organic farmers in Tamil Nadu, from whom reStore used to purchase millets, to grow organic cotton. The farmers were given seeds from our network of organic farmers with experts like Pamayan, an organic farmer and activist, helping get non-GMO seeds. They were of the species, hirsutum, the American cotton, and the farmers were trained to grow them organically. From the next year, we shifted our focus to the traditional Indian cotton varieties such as arboreum known as desi cotton. All over India, wherever desi cotton began to be grown, the associated traditional practices came back. For instance, desi cotton was always grown under mixed cropping, thus promoting food and commercial crops rather than just cotton. Thus along with desi cotton many other crops like coriander, chilly, onion, castor, millets and pulses were grown.

Another important point was that desi cotton was always short staple varieties, and amenable to hand processing only.

However, the machines (mostly imported from Britain earlier on, and later from Europe in general) were designed for the long staple American cotton. This added to the woes of revival of desi cotton as the industry was in favour of the long staple American cotton. Besides, with the American cotton came the American bollworm for which 50% of our input costs were spent on harsh chemical pesticides.

The Tula Philosophy

Tula came up as a sustainable initiative bringing together rainfed desi cotton growing farmers, skilled khadi spinners, master weavers, dyers who specialise in vegetable dyes, embroiders, and hand block printers as a decentralised model to create unique eco-friendly garments.

To minimise the carbon footprint and transport costs significantly, Tula follows a unique model of Cotton to Cloth within a respective state. For example, when cotton is sourced from Karnataka, the spinning, dyeing and weaving are done in and around the state. There have been some hiccups in subsequent years so that cotton, as yarn or lint, has been moved between states, and to farther locations, within the three states of Tamil Nadu, Karnataka, and Maharashtra, but, of course, for reasons of quality, business optimisation, and volumes.

Tula emphasizes on decently remunerating all the farmers and artisans involved in a fair and timely manner. Hence, Tula does not believe in credit system, so it neither takes nor gives any credit. There is an adherence to equity amongst all the players in making the garments, and unjustified profits have been eliminated. The distribution of income is based on the productivity of each of the players to earn a respectable livelihood using their skills.

Tula has worked with local communities in Tamil Nadu, Karnataka and Maharashtra. Each place grows their local, indigenous seeds, or some improved varieties of the same stabilised in the 1960s and '70s.

Future Plans

In the future I hope to help more people, especially the youth, to replicate such models that are ecologically and economically viable. We would also like to come up with new plant-based, eco-friendly fibres. Then we would also like to collaborate with technologists to create simple, small machines that can help the rural Indian woman process cotton, especially to convert lint to sliver/roving, which is the input for amber charkhas.

I am now also associated with the India HandMade Collective (IHMC) where we work with various groups working with primary artisans making handmade artisanal products, across India, to create a market. More generally, I would like to work on simple enterprises that are rural- and local-based. As part of the Non-Violent Economy Network (NVEN) we wish to promote and mentor small, local enterprises in rural India that can bolster the local rural economy.

❑❑❑

CHAPTER 9

Leveraging Opportunities Influenced my Life

Dr Deepti Omchery Bhalla

A Carnatic vocalist, Hindustani light music singer, and dancer of both the Kathakali and Mohiniattam dance forms. Dr Deepti Omchery Bhalla is a multi-faceted artiste. As an academician she melded her passion with academics. The performing artist did her BA, MA, MPhil and PhD in Carnatic music. Her research in the arts, both music and dance, of Kerala, led to the publishing of her book Vanishing Temple Arts. She began teaching in 1985, and was a senior professor, and dean and head of the department of music at the Faculty of Music and Fine Arts, University of Delhi, when she retired in 2022. Post retirement, she continues to passionately pursue her love of music.

My parents have been my greatest inspiration. My mother, Padma Shri Dr Leela Omchery, is an eminent musicologist. Though hailing from an illustrious family of musicians and teachers, she struggled hard in life to raise her two children, and follow her passion for music, which, she learnt right from her childhood, as part of her family tradition of learning music and dance as an essential part of life, with dedication and perseverance. And that is what finally led to her receiving the national recognition of being awarded the Padma Shri.

My father, Prof. Omchery NN Pillai, is an eminent Malayalam playwright. He comes from a humble background, and while struggling with several challenges that came his way as a child, youth and a parent too, he not only gained the respectability as an academician, but also pursued his passion for theatre. He was selected for doing his master's from Pennsylvania University, USA, and became the first professor of journalism and mass communication at the Indian Institute of Mass Communication, Delhi. Overcoming many hurdles, he also rose up to be a renowned playwright, becoming a winner of the Kendra Sahitya Akademi award for literature.

The Beginnings of the Performing Arts – Carnatic Music, Kathakali and Mohiniattam

Being born to such parents, who struggled to become achievers, was in itself a blessing for me, and my first step towards a purposeful life. Raising me in Delhi, away from the state of their origin, Kerala, did not deter my parents from inculcating in me the culture and traditions of Kerala. Malayalam was the language always spoken at home. Observing my talent in both music and dance, I was sent for training in Kathakali from

great masters of the dance form at the International Centre for Kathakali, New Delhi.

My mother was my first guru of music, who, besides teaching me Carnatic music, also found it necessary for me to learn important verses from the Vedas and the Upanishads; stotras; and Malayalam poetry of renowned poets of Kerala, all in melody, composed by her, which made it easier for me to learn and memorize.

My mother was very particular about my building up a strong foundation in both music as well as dance, for which she ensured I learnt from the best of gurus who were masters of their art. It was only learning and practise which was given importance in the beginning. Gradually the experience of performing on stage came in for me to overcome any inhibition or fear of failure in performance.

Having learnt Kathakali for twelve years under great masters, I went on to learn Mohiniattam under the legend, the late guru Kalyanikutty Amma. Though my Kathakali training helped me immensely in the execution of eye expressions and hand gestures, I also realized that my bold eye expressions and vigorous body movements acquired through this training were in opposition to the style which required just the opposite. Determined to work upon myself in overcoming this limitation, which took me almost a year, I travelled from Delhi to Kerala frequently for training under my guru, and worked on myself till my guru was satisfied with my restrained facial expressions and soft flowing body movements. This was a major change for which I worked hard for a whole year with constant practice of the same. A major challenge I faced was in my performance with a repertoire that was similar to another classical dance form of the South. Both being nurtured in the same region, and popularized in the courts of the Travancore maharajas, the similarity was only natural. My initial performances got many negative comments regarding the same, and no matter how much effort I made I was always subjected to criticism by some who felt my style to be a replica of the other classical dance form. Getting negative comments at the beginning of one's career can be very depressing, and it gave a sense of hopelessness, which was what I felt during those initial years of my struggle in establishing myself as a dancer. At one point I had even decided to give up my career as a dancer, and focus only on my music. It was my mother who found a solution which was of enhancing the repertoire with compositions that were different from the existing ones, found in the traditional music of Kerala. Together we unearthed several genres and musical forms which not only enhanced the existing repertoire, but also provided me the opportunity of exhibiting my potential and talent as a dancer. Thereafter there was no looking back. I further worked on its existing simple rhythmic structures with my knowledge of Carnatic classical music, incorporating complex rhythms from the traditional art forms of Kerala, which further added to its aesthetic appeal. The success at each point was not merely because of my passion, but also a sincere pursuit towards a definite goal, which was difficult yet achievable because of hard and persistent efforts that kept me going to finally contributing towards the development of the style.

To the tunes of Hindustani Music

I have also had my share of singing Hindustani music. I first started humming Hindustani music ragas listening to my mother's Hindustani music lessons at home when she trained under the veteran Pandit Pran Nath of the kirana gharana. I used to sing the *chota khyaal* taught to her. I started singing songs in children's programme at the age of 8, solo, and also along with three young singers who would become doyens of their gharanas – the late Ustad Iqbal Ahmed Khan of Delhi gharana, the late Pandit Jwala Prasad, and Ustad Mujahid Hussain Khan of Rampur gharana. The four of us would record

together for children's broadcasts. I started learning Hindustani light music under veteran composers of All India Radio (AIR), Delhi, like Pandit Shivprasad and Pandit Surendra Soni. I also learnt Hindustani classical music from Ustad Yunus Hussain Khan, a doyen of Agra gharana, while training in voice culture from the dhrupad maestro the late Faiyazuddin Dagar in Delhi. Hindustani ragas were not much known in Kerala in the 1980's, and I had the opportunity to render songs in ragas like todi, bhatiyar, and madhuvanti on AIR, Trivandrum, and on Doordarshan.

Pursuing Higher Education and Research in the Performing Arts

On the academic front, I pursued my higher education in Carnatic music from Delhi University. I did my BA, MA and MPhil in Carnatic music. I then went on to do my doctorate in Carnatic music. In the year 2006 I came out with my book *Vanishing Temple Arts* based on almost three-and-one-half decades of my research work. This research had inputs from my mother too. The research focused on the various arts – traditional music and dance – that existed in the temples of Kerala. More specifically, in the Kanyakumari district which was part of erstwhile Travancore, and now in the state of Tamil Nadu.

I researched on the kinds of folk music, the *sangeet natakas*, the *hari katha kalakshepams*, that existed in that time in the region of Kerala. I focused on the *sopana* music tradition, the temple music tradition, of Kerala. This is very different from the present-day Carnatic concert music that we listen to. I studied the distinctive features of *sopana* music, and how it commenced in the temples of Kerala. The ordering of presentation of *sopana* music was also part of my research. In the current times that order does not exist; it existed maybe till about 80 years ago. Also part of my research was some of the very rare *talas*, information about which was found in Tamil language, identified on old palm leaves. The reason why this is in Tamil is because the Malayalam script came much later; most of the script followed in the region of Kerala was Tamil, the ancient Tamil. The study of the musical instruments of Kerala was also part of my research.

I also researched on the dancers who were part of the temple rituals referred to as *thalinanka* or *nankaiyyar*. *Thali* means temple and *nanka* means dancer; *nankaiyyar* refers to a dancer whose hand gestures were very beautiful. There were different categories of dancers, and statuses were accorded to them accordingly.

In the context of the Mohiniattam dance form, I have researched considering three time periods taking as reference the period of Swathi Thirunal (1813 – 1846), the Maharaja of Travancore, who was a highly accomplished music composer and musician, and promoter of the arts. The Swathi period is the most important with regard to the development of Mohiniattam, as it was in this period that it got a concrete shape, structure, and repertoire. There is very fragmented information about the kind of music and dances that existed in the temples of Kerala in the pre-Swathi period. And in the post-Swathi period, the status of dancers degenerated because of the lack of royal patronage. The dancers had to somehow make a living by entertaining the local rich chieftains and general public. The forms of dance that developed in this period existed before they were completely banned by the British regime. Subsequently, they were revived in 1930 by Vallathol and Mukundaraja when they established the Kerala Kalamandalam.

Tracing the Roots

If I go back to the roots of the knowledge I acquired, that has been the basis of my research and my book, it is my parents I owe it to. My mother hails from Thiruvattar, also in the Kanyakumari district. The famous Adikeshava temple is situated in Thiruvattar. My maternal grandfather, as part of the temple managing committee, managed the temple services and other activities in the temples of Kanyakumari district that included Suchindram and Thiruvattar.

Well-known musicians of the early 19th century would come and perform in these temples. My grandfather eventually became the president of the managing committee of many of the small temples there. My mother could therefore have direct access to the musicians, and be acquainted with their singing styles. She could also sit with them for hours on end to learn music from them.

On my paternal side, my father hails from Vaikom, where the Kshetra Kala Peethom is into every kind of music and musical instruments connected with the temples of Kerala. When I was a young child my mother was doing research on *sopana sangeetam*. At that time veteran artistes and musicians from the Kshetra Kala Peethom would come to my father's place, quite late in the evening, and they would sit for long hours to discuss about *sopana sangeetam*. That is how my mother, an adept at both Carnatic and Kerala music, could understand and analyze *sopana* music. It, therefore, became a kind of an oral tradition for me to learn many aspects of *sopana sangeetam*, and many small songs, *dhyana shlokas*, and small devotional songs that my mother learnt from those eminent musicians from the past through the oral tradition. My doctoral research and my book are a reflection of what I learnt and understood both through the oral tradition as also my meetings and interaction with stalwarts like Neeleshwara Shankara Marar, and other great *sopana* singers and musicians.

❑❑❑

CHAPTER 10

For Moms and Dads and Kids

Sushant Kalra

After a bachelor's in metallurgical engineering from Jadavpur University, and a master's in finance from Delhi University, Sushant Kalra joined the corporate sector. Over time, ideas and ideals in the area of parenting started assuming greater and greater importance to him. He, therefore, quit his well-established corporate job to found the Parwarish Insitute of Parenting in 2008. He subsequently also earned a diploma in early childhood and education, as also a master's degree in education. He has authored the book Perfect Parenting – How to Raise Happy and Successful Children. Through his novel organization he has taken parenting and child development to a new level.

I never wanted to be a parent. Monica and I got married in the year 1995, and we were very clear that we would not have children. From there to parenting 24×7 for the past 12 years. It has been a roller coaster journey, a journey of desperation, frustration, fulfillment, satisfaction, fun, excitement, big failures and bigger jumps. If God asks me to go back and re-live my life from the start, I do not think I would want to make any change. I would re-live my life the way it has panned out.

Marriage and Parenthood

Our decision to not have children was based on logic and practicality. Having seen almost every parent around us struggle – the struggles of getting children to listen, eat, study, behave, perform, and on to monitoring their habits. The list from the parents was unending. From a child's point of view too all this does not make for a very happy, harmonious or loving time. Having your parents after you all the time is not a great experience as a child.

Armed with this knowledge and experience of parents and children around us, we were clear that we did not want to get into this trap, and we did not want to have a child too get into this trap.

But to marry and then to decide to not have children is almost an impossible task in our country. No one in the family and friends circle will let you be. So, after withstanding social pressures for 5 years, we gave in. Aman was born in June 2000. But we were clear that we did not want to go the same way every parent goes.

The Genesis of the Idea of Parwarish

And there began the idea of Parwarish - christened and registered 8 years later. The research, observations, thinking, reading, writing related to parenting, child development, and then the practising of those theories and beliefs became my passion. This resulted in the creation of a child development model based on the following belief:

Every child is born with all the power in the world. Born no-limit. And our role as a parent is to create a conducive environment where these powers are nurtured. (And not damaged because of our unconscious actions and conversations with them.)

Personal experiences and the results thereof emboldened us to take this process to others. The initial experiences and results with parents were extraordinary, leading to a cementing of the belief, or, rather, moving the belief system to something that "is".

Working as a vice president (field operations) at Max New Life Insurance, my career as a professional was going great at that point in time. And it was very natural to continue on the professional journey of growth in a sunrise industry. The money and the luxuries that such a position brings makes one fall into the trap of getting used to them, and they, eventually, become more of a need rather than a want. This is quite common.

Whilst my corporate career was going well, there was an experience of "being incomplete" every day. It was as if I was enjoying the journey, but the soul was somewhere not fulfilled. The thought that "this is not it" was lingering, and I was not able to crack it for years. I thus kept proceeding on the default journey.

My conversations with friends, trusted colleagues, and even my parents and spouse on this topic resulted in everyone saying: "This is the way it is supposed to be."

It was over a post-dinner discussion one day with a childhood friend, Gurmeet Singh, that I shared my idea that if it would be possible, I would want to support parents on their journey as parents. The issues parents are struggling with and the adverse impact it is having on children too, can be altered, and made good, I pointed out, and added that this was my dream. But given my educational qualifications of a bachelor's in engineering and master's in finance, and with 18 years of experience in the corporate world, I expressed my doubts in ever being able to fulfill this dream of mine.

To my surprise my friend asked me, "Do you want this to happen in reality?" And added, "Please do join the Landmark Forum, and I promise you that it will happen!"

The next morning, I went to Landmark Education's office, and registered for the 3-day Landmark Forum. It proved to be a personal transformational journey, and in the next year and a half reconstructed me. The barriers (at the level of truths) that I was carrying about myself and life got shattered, and a new Me emerged. Within six months of the process with Landmark education, I was leading my first program before thirty parents. The feedback from them and from a senior school principal ratified the belief system, and the parenting processes we had designed.

Landmark Education's learning experiences altered the view to life for me. It established two dictums, and also gave me the tools to make it happen.

The two dictums were:

I could do anything which I wanted in my life.

I can break every barrier coming in the way of my mission.

Quitting a Well-established Corporate Career to Pursue a Novel Initiative

It took me 2 years thereafter to gather the courage to quit my blooming corporate career, and convince my family to trust me, and to let me jump into the world of uncertainty, of creating from nothing. Setting up an organization in an industry which did not exist – starting a parenting training company. The Parwarish Institute of Parenting. With no prior experience or education in the area, starting off all alone with everyone around saying: "This is not possible".

But that statement from them, I guess, added fuel to the fire within me. I took the plunge, and resigned from my job against everyone's advice. The scariest thing which I ever did in my life.

Probably this madness of "doing my own thing, my way" was nurtured in me, and I was given that space during my childhood. Breaking stereotypes and norms was something I enjoyed during my childhood. Sometimes I got reprimanded for those antics, and a lot of times I got kudos for making something happen when it was not expected. Unconventional thinking and views were sometimes snubbed by the adults around, and a lot of times the out-of-the-box thinking met with appreciation.

The strong family values of love, care and compassion just naturally flowed into us from our parents and extended family. Putting people and relationships above luxuries and money were the foundation stones which got laid by the family long before we became conscious of these terms. Now, in my current capacity, I share with parents: Habits and values are never taught, they are caught!

The vision of empowering families had a strong foundation in "making a difference" and "compassion" which had become a part of me. The tenacity I observed in Mahatma Gandhi as I listened to, watched, and read about him inspired me to follow my dream: Let not anything stop you from your mission.

The Parwarish Institute of Parenting

The belief and the philosophy which got established for our first child was the seed of Parwarish. Experts from the areas of psychology, child development, childhood studies, and counselling joined in, and worked one on one with parents and children. We not only started to understand how and why parents think and behave in a particular way, but also how we can partner and empower parents to do that with their unique children in their unique environment. Every parent, every child, and every family environment, however similar they may look, is unique. One way, one style, even one style for one type does not work. This makes parenting a very complex social labyrinth.

Working closely with parents and children across the globe, across socio-economic strata, slowly and steadily built up the Parwarish Child Development Model. The continuous, slow, and gruelling sessions, discussions and debriefs led us into fine tuning the model. Years of extensive research and development resulted in the 'No limit Child program' which guarantees results to every family in 2 months.

I also came out with my book *Perfect Parenting – How to Raise Happy and Successful Children.* Written in a conversational style and in a layman's language, it provides parents with tools to create their own unique perfect blend of parenting. The book, published in 2021, seeks to break the myth that something like perfect parenting does not exist. Every parent is perfect, and every child is perfect too. And there is no one formula of parenting.

Additionally, I also upped my academic qualifications. I had done a bachelor's in engineering in the field of metallurgy from Jadavpur University, Kolkata, and a master's in finance from Delhi University, prior to starting my working life. After starting Parwarish I did a diploma course in early childhood and education, from the Indira Gandhi National Open University,

Delhi, and also earned a master's degree in education from the Jamia Milia Islamia, Delhi.

The past decade of building Parwarish as a philosophy more than a company or a brand has been the most fulfilling journey as a professional, as a father, and, most importantly, as a human being for me.

Starting off as one who was unknown in the field of child development many a milestone has been achieved over the years. More than two-hundred-and-fifty thousand parents across the globe have been empowered through Parwarish. I have been invited to speak on the TEDx platform multiple times. Awards have also come my way such as the Education Innovator Award, and the Courageous Class Award, besides others.

Parwarish is on its mission to make parenting a fulfilling and joyful experience for parents who are raising no-limit children to grow up to be no-limit adults.

❑❑❑

CHAPTER 11

There is Nothing Like Life

Shehla Hashmi Grewal

From theatre to academics and back to theatre. Shehla Hashmi Grewal was a co-founder of the Jana Natya Manch (Janam), a theatre group. She then went in for teaching as a career after doing a master's program in regional development. She taught geography at school level in Delhi. Subsequently, she gave up teaching at school to go back and pursue her love of theatre. She also began engaging in various activities to educate and spread awareness among children and the young. She also learnt the art of pottery, and now runs a studio where she also teaches the craft.

Partition of our country forced hundreds of thousands of our country men and women to go through unimaginable miseries. These included losing one's near and dear ones, as also land

and property, and being cruelly displaced from that which had been their homes for several generations. This was the end result of 200 years of British colonial rule. Families were divided, and many were left alone to fend for themselves.

The Family's Troubled Beginnings

Among the affected was also my father who refused to leave his motherland – India. On the other hand, my mother, whose family moved to Pakistan, came back to India in February 1949 to get married to my father. They started their married life together in the Kashmiri Gate area of Delhi where my father had a prosperous furniture business. Their happiness was, however, short-lived. The heightened communal tensions that gripped North and North-West India including Delhi at that time led to the collapse of my father's business. This brought the family face to face with poverty. By the time I was born, in 1952, as the third among five siblings, our house was without power and water supply as bills could not be paid. These were tough times for my family. At times we could not get even two square meals to eat.

The Opportunity to Holistic Education

Despite this our parents ensured our education, and involved us in several creative activities including poetry reading, story-telling, putting up small skits, painting, and many other activities. They also made it a point to regularly relate to us things as diverse as the saga of our freedom struggle, European paintings and sculptures, and astronomy. This positive attitude and determination in the face of adversity helped us all, in large

measure, to overcome the negative impact of poverty. In the long run these childhood experiences helped broaden our intellectual horizons, and steeled us in facing up to the adversities that we encountered in our adult lives. They also brought home to me the importance of a multi-faceted education of children. However, I was able to appreciate the real value of such an education only after I became a teacher.

A Career in Teaching

I started my teaching career as a geography teacher after finishing my master's in regional development from the Jawaharlal Nehru University, Delhi. My first assignment was

at the Sacred Heart College in Dalhousie. This was followed by teaching nursery classes for a few months at the Guru Harkishan Public School in Delhi. As teaching at school level requires a BEd degree, I went in for doing the course. On completing it I joined Sardar Patel Vidyalaya (SPV), Delhi. While teaching at SPV, I started taking bi-weekly classes for economically deprived minority community girls at Nizamuddin Basti in Delhi. These girls had a strong desire to study, but did not have the means to receive education in their mother tongue. For these classes I had to brush up my Urdu. It was such a joy to look at the faces of these girls, and their bright eyes opening wide with each new bit of information. Many of these girls could eventually get out of the shackles of backwardness and become financially independent women. The story of these women and the organisation, Seher, was written by Shobha Menon in 2019 as a book titled, *Resilience – The Story of Muslim Women.* I feel till we succeed in educating and liberating women, 50% of our creativity and productivity remains unachieved. During this period I also wrote some lessons for Open School students.

Coming Full Circle: Back to Theatre

I enjoyed teaching at the school, but its demands were such that I could not get time to pursue many of my other interests. These included theatre. I had been involved with Jana Natya Manch (Janam) since its inception in 1973, as one of the founding members. Janam later turned into a major street theatre group. A regular teaching job, and two little children did not give me time to be active in theatre for nearly a decade.

In 1992 I took a very tough decision of leaving my job, which was my bread and butter. My husband was very supportive of my embarking on this new path. To begin with, I got busy writing adult literacy primers in Hindi for the Delhi Saksharta Samiti. At the same time I tried to become actively involved with my theatre group. I did not do as much acting as I had done during the early days of Janam. Besides acting, I found back-stage work to be very interesting. As a result I played a major role in doing the costumes for stage plays like *Varun ke Betey, Moteram ka Satyagraha, Satyashodhak, Ma,*

Hipashia, and *Char Rang*, besides others. I also created props for both stage and street plays for more than two decades. This work was voluntary, and did not pay me anything. Nonetheless, I thoroughly enjoyed this work. I see this as my little effort to make people aware of the reality, and open some windows to fresh ideas.

Engaging in Sensitizing and Creating Awareness

I was not alone in this endeavour. Many others with whom I worked shared the same vision. We worked together not just in creating plays, but also in diverse activities whether it was arranging to facilitate children to witness a solar eclipse, or writing adult literacy primers. For instance, a total solar eclipse occurred in the year 1995. Due to superstitions and lack of awareness, misinformation regarding the eclipse was rampant in Delhi's slums. I saw this as an opportunity to let the disadvantaged children of these colonies know the real geographical and scientific reasons for the occurrence of an eclipse. For this purpose I joined the Delhi Gyan Vigyan Samiti. We, as a group, started organizing workshops for local schools, and educating them about solar eclipses. I, along with a friend, wrote a booklet on how to watch the eclipse safely and without harming one's eyes. This booklet was appreciated by children and teachers alike. We were successful in having children watch the eclipse with special UV filter paper spectacles. We distributed thousands of such spectacles. We also took many busloads of people to Bharatpur, where the visibility of the eclipse was much better than in Delhi. This was an amazing time. So many like-minded, educated people were working together to watch a beautiful celestial phenomenon, and spread awareness among people.

So, along with regular school education, I could see the scope of spreading awareness through informal means. I also realised that each one of us has different abilities which can be utilised for the purpose. Completing school and college education is one thing, one stage of education, but liberating the mind and being able to think logically and freely, and question the status quo is quite another. To my mind the latter is more important for the development of society. Whether you teach geography, English, art or sculpture what is important is the motive in your mind. Advancement of the collective human knowledge, and using it for the advancement of the human race - this, in my understanding, is education. I do not miss any opportunity to do my bit to advance this goal, especially among younger children. To this end I have written books on diverse topics like travel, craft, and cooking. Besides this, I have written geography primers for Delhi's middle schools; ICSE geography text books for the ninth and tenth grades; and a series of resource material for the University School Resource Network Project sponsored by the Ratan Tata Trust.

Quite late in my life I realised that I am a dyslexic. All my life I have been facing problems in reading, spelling, and writing, and as a result I was always self-conscious of writing in front of people, and on the blackboard in school! I compensated that with my teaching techniques, and gave my best to the students. I had to work much harder than many others as I had to write and rewrite everything many times for it to be presentable. In those days these learning problems were not understood that well, and many of us were not even aware of them. Even today I have these difficulties, but writing many times over is like breathing for me. It does not bother me in any way.

Sometime during this period one of my old students from Nizamuddin Basti called me up. She, after her further education, had brought up her children single-handedly. She had opened a small centre *Pehchan* for girls who were in the same situation in which she had been two decades earlier. She wanted me to take their geography classes. Her centre is located in Jaitpur in South-East Delhi while I live in Gurgaon. I had no heart to say no to her. So I started going there twice a week. Today many *Pehchan* girls are professionals and gainfully employed young women.

Crafting with Clay

In the year 1995, I started learning the art and craft of pottery from a renowned studio potter of our country, Devi Prasad. After finishing my course with him, I set up my own studio, and by 1999 I started taking classes. Now I have been teaching pottery for more than twenty years. Each day in my studio is fascinating. Teaching pottery, and creating with clay is an amazing process, and is tremendous fun. Being a craft, the more we engage in pottery, the more we improve at it, and it also keeps one on one's toes. The computer has opened such a vast field in the area of pottery that one feels like a midget.

I still want to learn so much, do so much, but time is running out. What I feel is important is that we have to learn to appreciate and acknowledge the contribution of generations of humans - past and present, and pass on all that is positive in our ethos to the coming generations.

❑❑❑

CHAPTER 12

The Un-becoming Way

Lakshmi Menon Bhatia

With a bachelor's degree in psychology, and a master's degree in social work, Lakshmi Menon Bhatia has worked in varied areas. She worked as a counsellor, as an anchor person with Doordarshan, and with mobile creches. She was also associated with the Salaam Balak Trust. She served as the global director of the American clothing company, Gap Inc. She was also involved in facilitating the setting up of Women in Value Chains. She has conducted meditation and self discovery workshops. She has a deep interest in the spiritual and mystical. Currently she runs Terrace Stories sourcing the material for the bouquets and eco-friendly gifts that she makes from her flourishing terrace garden.

"We shall not cease from exploration/ And the end of all our exploring/Will be to arrive where we started/And know the place for the first time." This quote from TS Eliot is a favourite of mine. It, in a way, describes my life which feels like a spiral. And it is something like this: You keep meandering through life, life happens to you, and you feel many times you are coming back to the same point, but maybe with a deeper understanding about life, about yourself, and your relationship with the world around.

The Influence of School and College Years

I hail from Kerala, but grew up in Delhi. My father worked in the government in the field of education. My mother was a teacher. She taught mathematics at Carmel Convent School, the same school that I went to. My childhood was fairly simple. But I always used to wonder about the greater existential issues of life. Even as a young child I used to feel old. My questions were all about what the purpose of life is, who I am, why I am here, why the world is the way it is, and so on. I would spend endless hours during my school years sitting on the terrace of my home just staring at the clouds, and many times making up stories. I guess I lived in the stories I created in my mind. Imagination in those years used to be my escape route as well as my strength.

I was quite an introvert as a youngster. But music, and then eventually, debating and quizzing helped me come out of my shell. I was very fortunate to have teachers and mentors who took a lot of interest in my development. I was really blessed to have their guidance to become more confident as I grew up.

School life was fun with a great deal of activities, including extra-curricular activities such as music. The Carmelite nuns were highly supportive, and gave us a lot of freedom and space to be ourselves. I also went on to become the head girl at school.

I did my graduation in psychology from the Jesus and Mary College in Delhi. College life was just a continuation of the blast that I used to have in my later years in school. I became the college president too. I got a number of cultural activities going thanks to this, and it was a lot of fun.

Entering the World of Social Work and Counselling

After graduating in psychology, in 1992, I felt I was getting too analytical. I needed to ground myself a bit more. So I went in for doing my master's in social work from the Delhi School of Social Work, Delhi University. That was a practical grounding course because 3 days of the week we had lecture classes and the remainder 2 days we did field work. That was when I started working with Salaam Balak Trust, and the street children, which helped me connect closely with the issues of migrants which would help me later on in the work I was meant to do.

I also started working with Doordarshan. I was already engaging with All India Radio. At Doordarshan I started working as an anchor for a live show. I also made documentaries, put together modules, and did interviews of artistes and celebrities.

Life was full and rich. Today when I look at the world around me, and the lives of a lot of children of the current generation I feel they do not have the vast openness to experience, experiment and explore the different facets of life. And sometimes individuals become highly monochromatic. I say this because I have been into counselling for a number of years, having trained as a counsellor. I see that children have really not been given the space or the bandwidth because of the pressures of education, parental pressure, the need to conform. And I compare this with the kind of freedom many of us experienced when we were growing up. School and college were the most amazing years where one could just be. My parents, teachers and mentors were supportive, open, and empowering. I am grateful to them for moulding me, and making me what I am.

After my master's in social work (MSW) I worked at Jesus and Mary College as the student counsellor for two years. Then came marriage. Thereafter I started working with mobile creches which again brought me into the heart of working with issues of migrants and workers on construction sites. I was heading their fundraising and communications function, and there was a lot of learning there.

This was followed by a stint in St Columba's School, Delhi, as the school social worker in their middle school for a year or so.

Donning Multiple Hats in the Corporate Sector

It was during this time that I was contacted by Gap Inc, an American clothing company. They were looking for somebody who could look at labour issues, and do labour audits in the factories they were sourcing from. I landed myself the job. And it took me on a fifteen-year journey initially looking after North India and Nepal, and eventually becoming their global director looking after their strategic partnerships globally. I had a team in the Americas, Asia, Europe and Africa reporting in to

me. I travelled to more than 30 countries for a decade. For around 200 days a year I used to be out of the country. I travelled so much, learnt so much, saw so much through all of this - in conflict situations; in supply chain disputes between factory managements; in terrible accidents in the factories from where sourcing happened. While I worked on difficult issues, I was fortunate that I was able to see, understand and leverage the power of partnerships. Though wearing a corporate hat, I was working closely with the United Nations, particularly the International Labour Organization (ILO), and United Nations Office on Drugs and Crime (UNODC); with trade union leaders; with global NGOs; and with other corporations. I was on the board of the Ethical Trading Initiative in the UK for a number of years learning how tripartite structures can work, engaging closely with governments in countries such as Bangladesh, Turkey, Lesotho, Egypt, Bahrain, and the UK. There was a lot of work related to the press, and I used to be a spokesperson on certain issues related to ethical supply chain for Gap.

Parallelly, a deeper seeking began. Also 9/11 was a wake-up call for the world. It impacted me deeply personally for a number of reasons. The deeper search really began from there. The next decade that I continued to be with Gap I was travelling a lot. I could see the underlying thread of unity, that for human beings, despite all other identities, the identity of humanity is the deepest. It is what connects us all. The joys, the sorrow, the pain, the longing, the loss, the struggles are all common threads which I saw across the world. Therefore, I used to feel at home wherever I went. I truly felt I was a global citizen, and any lesser identity was a bit of a struggle.

The Inner Spiritual Search

From the year 2012, I was on the next phase of my life which was about my inner searching and inner seeking. The pendulum swung to the other side, so to say. And then I got back into counselling and soul coaching, working with individuals, particularly women and children; and conducting meditation sessions and workshops on self-discovery.

But somewhere I knew my own search was incomplete, my own understanding was not adequate. I was also going through a lot of issues including those related to health. And then I was very fortunate to meet my living guru, Sri M. I have received the grace, guidance and blessings of Sri M, and many masters before that – too many to name, and I am grateful to all the masters.

The next phase of my journey has been about knowing myself better. I am beginning to realize that it is indeed our inner reality which manifests outside. As Karl Jung has said it so beautifully that what we see outside is just a manifestation of the collective consciousness. I believe that if we want to see a better world, if we want more peace and harmony, we, each of us, will have to find that space within us. Where I am now is to find that space within me where I can be deeply anchored so that what I put out and offer in the world is of a higher vibration, harmonious, peaceful, and comes from the vibration of love. Love and joy, I believe, are of the highest frequencies.

A Bouquet of Interests and Activities

At present I work in the area of business and human rights. Working on issues around women and livelihoods, in the apparel industry, I was able to facilitate the setting up of a network called Women in Value Chains which is an amalgamation of organizations that work on issues of women and livelihoods particularly in the informal parts of the supply chain. I also work in the field of music, art and culture, curating events which bring together everything from natural food, to understanding the interconnectedness between all of life, to poetry, music and art.

Just over a year ago, after the onset of the Covid-19 pandemic, my daughter and I felt the need to spread greater positivity. I live in a small apartment with a lot of plants on the terrace. And so we set up the Terrace Stories, where we put together, for birthdays, anniversaries, and such like events, bouquets and gifts which are earth-friendly. Indeed, one needs to thank Mother Nature who is so magnificent, keeps us all going, and gives us so much.

I believe that we are at the cusp of a great transformation as a species. As they say crisis precedes transformation. The pandemic and everything else are just the opening of a doorway through which we will have to walk through boldly. In order to do that we will have to transform ourselves. It will have to be a higher consciousness that can pass through into this different way of being. Perhaps that is why we see an increased interest in spirituality everywhere, with more and more people searching deeply for the meaning of life.

In my understanding the future belongs to communities of people who are able to bond at a deep heart and soul level; work together; share resources instead of having an I, me, myself approach; be sensitive to each other, to other species, and to the environment; and live according to their need, and not their greed. We are in the midst of that transformation of consciousness.

I like to refer to Einstein who said that the solutions for the problems that we see around us can never be at the same level of consciousness that created them in the first place. This essentially means that if we do not raise our consciousness, if we do not raise the bar, we will not have better results, greater results. There is a sense of urgency for us all to find and reclaim that space within of inner peace and harmony. Our work, our relationships, whatever we co-create, all need to come from that balanced, harmonized space inside of us. In order to do that a lot of our conditioning and judgement has to be let go off.

❑❑❑

CHAPTER 13

From the Science of Life to the Life of Art

Simi Rajan

After earning a bachelor's degree and a master's degree in botany from the Ranchi University, Simi Rajan went on to do a BEd program. And she went in for a career in teaching. She taught science and biology for students of the sixth to tenth grades in a school in Delhi. Thereafter, when she moved to Kerala, she changed course, and took to learning mural art. She has, for the past few years, been deeply involved in creating murals that are executed with great detail and are attractive in colour. Her murals can be seen at places around the country.

Success is both fleeting and constant. It comes in many forms, and at different times in life. The definition of success and achievement also evolves over time. As I look back, I think of success as the culmination of all the moments and experiences that have given me happiness, a sense of purpose, and desire to do more.

My Career as a Teacher

I was brought up in Ranchi, Jharkhand. I did my schooling in St. Joseph's High school, and did my BSc and MSc in botany from the Ranchi University. I was truly passionate about botany as a subject, and it culminated in my teaching biology after completing my BEd program with English and science.

My career as a teacher in Delhi spanned fifteen years with 1800-plus middle school students, and it brought me joy and a sense of accomplishment. I taught science for the sixth, seventh and eighth grades, and biology for the ninth and tenth grades. As a teacher I always tried to go beyond the textbook, and help my students understand the fundamentals of biology through experiments and interactive diagrams. I am also passionate about creating awareness on the issue of climate change, and tried to inculcate a similar passion and sense of urgency for protecting our planet among my students through awareness drives, recycling campaigns, and other organized efforts. As a class teacher, I would often get the most challenging of students, and I would take extreme pride and pleasure in making a positive impact in their lives and outlook. I have followed the careers of several of my past students, and I love connecting with them. Just like my family's success, I believe the success of my students complements mine.

Changing Course – Pursuing Mural Art Making

I truly learnt the meaning of evolving success when I made a pivot from teaching at school level to pursuing art, and successfully converted my passion into a career. I realized in the process that it is never too late to follow one's passion. After having painted as a leisure activity for several years, I made a concerted effort in 2015 to learn the art of mural painting. Murals are one of the oldest art forms that humans have engaged in. In Kerala, murals depicting Hindu mythologies used to be painted across temple walls and palaces, and enjoyed royal patronage.

I studied mural painting under several esteemed artists - George Fernandez, KU Krishnakumar, and Prince Thonnakal - to learn different techniques, and define my own brand and style in the mural art world. I also studied at the Institute of Mural Painting at Guruvayur Temple which teaches through the traditional *gurukula* system.

Since 2015, I have created more than 30 mural art works which are now housed in museums, as for instance the Bhopal Museum; in institutes such as the Chandragupta Institute of Management; in hotels; and in homes of both loved ones and strangers. They also found a place in the movie superstar Chiranjeevi's home. These paintings have also been displayed at several prestigious venues such as at Delhi's India Habitat Center.

I love paintings that depict love and joy, and often find myself painting the duo of Radha and Krishna, or Baby Krishna. Recently, I also created a rare collection of murals depicting the Ramayana's Sunderkand and Dashavatara. One of my favourite paintings is the depiction of the first meeting between Sita and Hanuman. To me it symbolizes happier times to come. While the process of creating these paintings is in itself a source of joy for me, I feel overjoyed to see how they are received and looked after by others. It is my legacy that will survive in places both near and far.

The Making of Murals

Mural paintings as one of the oldest art forms began as cave paintings. The mural paintings that I am most inspired by are the old traditional paintings depicting Hindu mythologies painted across temple walls and palaces in Kerala. In fact, the first time I visited Guruvayur temple in 1990, I was so overwhelmed by the sheer magnificence of the paintings that I vowed to someday learn the art of mural paintings.

Making a mural painting is a test of love and patience. It generally takes me 3 to 4 weeks to complete a painting 5 feet by

4 feet in size. However, it took me up to 3 months to complete a more complex set of paintings - the depiction of the Sunderkand. Creating a mural always begins with the inspiration either from the person who is requesting the painting, or something that catches my eye. When I consult with the buyer, I often provide recommendations on themes or ways to make certain paintings

better based on my research and creative take. Note that all my original paintings have been on canvas, but someday I would like to try to do a painting on a wall. Murals are usually taken to be art made on walls. Murals however may be made on canvas, for instance. Mural painting, in fact, is also a style of painting. The primary advantage of canvas painting is that it can be done at a convenient place comfortably, and can then be planted on the wall. Moreover, it is possible to sell the art works done on canvas to a wider clientele.

Now for the various steps when I create a mural. Once I have an idea of the final image, I draw the intended picture on the canvas with a simple HB pencil. After outlining the image, I use acrylic paints to fill in. Sanskrit texts discuss in detail the style and effectiveness of the 5 dominant colours in mural paintings: scarlet red, Prussian blue, sap green, yellow ochre, and black. You will notice that my paintings reflect and balance the five colours. However, if other colours are desired, I usually mix two to three of the five colours to create a unique variation. After outlining the murals, we usually make the ornaments first, then the dress or outfit and surroundings. At the very end, we fill in the face and figure. The face especially is crucial to make sure that emotions are adequately reflected. After a painting is complete, I use black ink to outline the painting. This step is critical, and adds a very polished look to the painting, and adds a significant amount of impact. The instruments used are simple - long hairbrushes, acrylic paint tray, paints, and water - but the impact is very rewarding. It is also important to be patient as the drawings are very fine, and sometimes a single part of the painting can take a long time given the inordinate detailing. I also listen to what my body and mind want - on some days I can sit and paint for hours, and on other days I need to disengage from the process to rejuvenate.

While painting, I enjoy listening to spiritual songs as they have an uplifting effect, and keep me motivated. I often add my own take to the theme and the painting by adding details to it. If I have to do a particularly difficult part of the painting, I spend several moments contemplating on how best to achieve it, often thinking about it during my prayer time. Thinking about the painting feels meditative, and praying over it has led to many successful outcomes and bouts of inspiration. I am thankful to God for continuing to motivate me to do my best, and to motivate me to continue bringing beautiful paintings to life.

Balancing Work and Family

Early in life I lost my mother. I was one of four sisters. I had to manage both home and school. This is when I learnt to balance work with passionately caring for my family, and this became a driver of my future achievements, post-marriage too. My husband has also been a big contributor to my success. He has been supportive of my dreams and career, and is a true partner in every way. Sheryl Sandberg, chief operating officer at Facebook, and an inspiration to many women leaders, had once famously said that the most important career choice you can make – especially as a woman – is who you choose to marry. My husband encouraged me to pursue my career in teaching. He also helped me pivot full-time from teaching to my passion in art. He continues to beam at my success, and comfort me in hardships. Together, we have also raised two daughters who we are proud of. My family's achievements – my husband's career,

and my daughters' education and careers – add to my joys and success. I have encouraged both my daughters to follow what they are passionate about, and find their own definition of success.

The beauty of success is that it is for you to define. To me, success is defined by both my own achievements that have brought me fulfilment and happiness as well as the success and contributions of the lives I have impacted. I am truly grateful that I have had the opportunity to experience and savour success on both counts, and I look forward to advancing both in the coming years.

❑❑❑

CHAPTER 14

A Rollercoaster Ride of Reinventing Myself

Dr Anjali Pathak

After earning a PhD in ancient Indian history and archaeology, Dr Anjali Pathak changed course. She trained to become a naturopath and healer, and began practising. She also went in to study and practise the organic farming science known as vrikshayurveda, and shared this knowledge with farmers and tea planters. She has authored the book Annam Brahma: Organic Food in India. She now runs Hariyaali Organics selling specialty teas under the brand name Peyaa.

What amazing surprises life holds for us if only we allow ourselves to be surprised in the first place. Entering the business world as a small-scale entrepreneur at an age when most of

my contemporaries are hanging up their boots, and bidding goodbye to their working life, has surely to be a curious saga.

As a student I was good at academics. As I pursued my higher education, I decided I would go in for teaching, and become a college/ university professor. I graduated from Delhi University, went on to do my masters from the Jawaharlal Nehru University, Delhi, and then headed to USA, on a scholarship, for my doctoral research. When I returned to India in the early 1990s, little did I realize that my whole world was going to be turned upside down because of unexpected, unanticipated changes.

From the Dream of Academia to Training to be a Naturopath

My dream of joining academia was shattered despite earning a PhD in ancient Indian history and archaeology. In fact, it had become just a worthless piece of paper in the end. And so, as I had always been interested in the healing arts, I trained as a healer and a naturopath, and set up a small practice in my hometown, Lucknow. This lasted for a few years, but could not continue for long as I lacked the business savvy to make money from fleecing patients. However, I soon realized that most of the patients I was offering consultation to were sick and miserable due to their poor diets and faulty lifestyles. So, until these aspects were rectified they could not hope for a lasting solution to their health issues. It also made me realize that farmers needed to grow pesticide-free food, and practice organic farming so that people everywhere – whether rural or urban - could have access to it. I, therefore, gravitated towards organic farming, and taught myself the basics of organic farming.

The Ancient Science of Vrikshayurveda

I studied vrikshayurveda, in particular, and practiced it in my own small garden. I also started writing about these organic farming practices in agricultural journals and magazines. What is vrikshayurveda? It is the ancient Indian science of farming, at least eleven thousand years old, if not more. A thousand years ago, Surapala composed a series of Sanskrit shlokas describing the salient features of vrikshayurveda. But this knowledge was lost during the following centuries. In the 1990s this ancient Sanskrit text was re-discovered and translated from Sanskrit into English, Hindi and other Indian languages. This translated text was the basis for my work on organic farming, and the results I came up with astonished everyone.

Destiny soon took me to the North East, and I came into contact with tea planters and small tea producers who had read my articles. I shared my knowledge with them, and started conducting organic farming workshops for small tea growers in Assam. Soon I was invited by large tea gardens as well

who wanted to convert their tea gardens to organic ones. My interaction with the tea industry in north-east India showed me how brutally the land had been treated by the use of chemical fertilizers and pesticides. With the use of vrikshayurveda methods of farming it became evident that all pesticide residues from the soil could be eliminated within three to six months. The inputs or expenditure on this transformation was minimal as vrikshayurveda uses locally available materials to improve farm output. I also realized that the CTC tea we take for granted, and drink unthinkingly, contained pesticide residues which were affecting our health in the long run. I wrote about various aspects of organic farming and organic tea cultivation in journals of the Indian tea industry. My foray into the interior regions of the North East also brought me in contact with a number of small farmers in Assam, Arunachal Pradesh, and Meghalaya. I shared my knowledge in the area of organic farming with them freely.

My travels all over India, and interaction with various organic farmers and retailers led me to compile a book on organic food. Titled *Annam Brahma: Organic Food in India*, it was published in the year 2009. The survey I conducted to compile this book brought me in contact with organic farmers, researchers and sellers all over India. It was seen that organic farming had taken off in the states of south India as well as in western India – Maharashtra and Gujarat. Therefore, organic shops and sellers had proliferated in south India as well as in western India. In north India as well as in eastern India the organic movement was very feeble or non-existent. The experiences of various organic farmers as well as organic retailers all over India were included in my book. In fact, I continue to remain in touch with these torch bearers of the organic movement right from Ladakh in the north to Kanyakumari in the south. My website, www.naturalorganicfarming.com, was also launched in the year 2012.

Meanwhile, I was compelled to close down my physical clinic due to my travels, but I continued to advise patients, especially cancer patients, over the phone and via e-mail. My own understanding of healing diseases like cancer and diabetes deepened with time. I also experimented with cannabis medicine, and found it to be greatly effective in treating not only cancer but also other chronic diseases like diabetes, arthritis, Alzheimer's, autism, epilepsy and so on. A website, www.healingcancerwithnature.com, was launched in 2015.

Setting up Hariyaali Organics

In my home garden I was also growing vishalata or sabah snake grass, a herbaceous plant, which has proven to be very effective as a supplement for cancer patients as also patients of other chronic diseases. My growing conviction that this herb be made available to a wider audience led me to set up a small limited liability company in late-2019. I christened the company Hariyaali Organics. But soon after the launch of my company, and a few products were readied for the market, the Covid-19 pandemic struck. With the moral support of my family I managed to keep my head above water in 2020 and 2021.

I am now learning about selling through e-commerce platforms, and honing my business skills in the process. I am also learning how to use the various social media platforms like facebook, instagram and youtube.

My line of herbal teas or tisanes under the brand name of Peyaa is now available for sale on e-commerce platforms such as Amazon, Flipkart, Qtrove, Shophealthy, and Lucknow Farmers Market. The herbs for Peyaa are sourced from small, organic farmers in Uttarakhand, Himachal, Ladakh and the Nilgiris. Seabuckthorn leaves, rose geranium leaves, butterfly pea flower (*aparajita*), rhododendron flowers and sabah snake grass are some of the unique ingredients that have been used in these tisanes.

I continue to advise patients all over India on phone and e-mail, and am now a member of the Society of Cannabis Clinicians, USA. Several patients who consulted me and followed my advice were able to defeat cancer and lead normal, healthy lives.

This roller coaster ride has taught me to be flexible in my approach. I had always wanted to be an entrepreneur, but earlier the conditions were just not right for me to take the plunge into the business world. Hariyaali Organics is now poised to take flight as soon as the Indian economy gets back on track after the Covid pandemic. But making money is not the only thing, or even the most important motive, in setting up this small-scale business. I am providing employment to a few local people, and encouraging some small organic farmers as well. Besides the activities that I engage in related to my business, several people continue to connect with me for information about organic farming practices, which I provide. And several people also contact me for the treatment of chronic diseases, especially cancer.

The most wonderful thing about keeping myself meaningfully occupied is that I hardly feel my age to be a limiting factor. I keep myself fit by eating healthy and exercising, and by going for detoxification and body tone up at various nature cure centres. I have always loved travelling, and look forward to resuming my travels after the Covid pandemic has sorted itself out. People my age are retiring or have retired, but I am just beginning my journey in the business world. My faith in the Universe, and my confidence in my innate abilities have brought me this far. My family has been my pillar of strength, and my support during all these years. Life is beautiful if only we allow ourselves to be awed by nature and the Universe.

❑❑❑

CHAPTER 15

Journeys in the Wilderness

Dr AJT Johnsingh

His passion for nature and wildlife, right from his childhood, saw Dr AJT Johnsingh making this his profession. His study of and research on the dhole, the Asiatic wild dog, a first of its kind, in the Bandipur Tiger Reserve, earned him a PhD degree. He also had a research stint in USA. A naturalist and field biologist, he worked at the Bombay Natural History Society. Thereafter he served as faculty at the Wildlife Institute of India for twenty years till 2005 when he retired as the dean, Faculty of Wildlife Sciences. He has the credit of walking the biodiversity-rich Western Ghats on foot. His travels into various wildlife areas, over the years, have translated into books authored by him. A dedicated conservationist, he has actively pursued

his passion post-retirement too. He is currently based in Bengaluru, and is associated with WWF-India, Nature Conservation Foundation, and The Corbett Foundation.

Memories of my early boyhood are full of scenes from my native village Anaigudi, where my paternal grandparents lived, at the southern tip of India. The bluish-green sea with its white spiraling wave-crests lapped at the black rocks, then frothed and rolled onto the sandy shore; red sand dunes with palmyrah palm and ficus trees stretched from the sea to the village; fan-throated lizards scurried along the sand dunes; and the cooing sounds of ring doves and calls of grey francolins echoed through the landscape.

Forays into the Wild

My schooling was in Nanguneri, at the Sankar Reddiar Board High School, where my parents were serving as teachers. The medium of instruction was Tamil. Nanguneri is in the rainshadow of the Kalakad Hills, a part of the Western Ghats, which form part of the present day Kalakad-Mundanthurai Tiger Reserve. Hunting was then allowed, and my father used to get small-game license paying a yearly fee of Rs 3000. The three of us - my brothers and I, used to thus hunt grey francolins, hares, ducks and teals. Fishing with simple home-made equipment in the nearby waterbodies was one of our favourite hobbies. Two of our country-bred dogs were our valuable companions on our hunting expeditions. Our interest in animals and hunting grew significantly once we had read Jim Corbett's *Man-Eaters of Kumaon*, in the Tamil, titled *Kumaum Puligal*, by T.J. Ranganathan. And our conversations often centered around

man-eating tigers, and the huge mahseer fishes Jim Corbett had caught.

What also importantly brought us close to wildlife and nature was our occasional camping trips to the nearby Kalakad Hills. We would go with our father and some friends. Sometimes my mother and two sisters too accompanied us, and we would stay in the abandoned staff quarters in the forest boundary built by the British. When the group was only of men and boys, we often stayed in the jungle itself camping on large flat rocks in the middle of the rivers. We always informed the local range forest officer about our trip when we set off. Sometimes we shot a jungle fowl or a hare or a mouse deer for the pot. After reading Jim Corbett's man-eater stories our trips to the jungle became very exciting as we imagined man-eating tigers and leopards behind every rock and bush, and, out of fear of attracting them, our conversations around the camp fire was in subdued tones.

Study and Research on Wildlife in their Habitats

A major turning point in my life was a meeting with the late JC Daniel, who would go on to become the director of the Bombay Natural History Society, in the year 1971, at the Kalakad Hills. When he found that I had a master's degree in zoology from the Madras Christian College (where he too had studied), and that I was teaching in Ayya Nadar Janaki Ammal (ANJA) College, Sivakasi, he encouraged me to take up research on wildlife. In due course he also helped me in my study of dholes, the Asiatic wild dogs, in the Sigur forests near the Mudumalai Wildlife Sanctuary in the company of Dr Michael Fox from USA. This study was my first introduction to a high-density elephant habitat where I learnt the art of walking in elephant jungle territory, sometimes even alone.

My research in the Sigur forests was followed by a two-year field study on dholes, towards my PhD, in the Bandipur Tiger Reserve. Financial support for my study came from WWF-India. Daniel was instrumental in arranging the permission for my field research, and the fund. While at Bandipur, another remarkable turning point in my life was the meeting with Dr John F Eisenberg from the Smithsonian Institution, USA. Seeing my interest in wildlife, and finding that I needed more training related to wildlife, he promised me a fellowship to undergo training with Dr John Seidensticker, who had studied tigers and leopards in Asia, in the Conservation and Research Center, a field station of the Smithsonian Institution, at Front Royal about 100 km from Washington D.C.

The Smithsonian Institution also arranged permission and travel money for my wife and five-year old son. As part of this 18-month training, during 1981-82, I capturcd and radio-tracked raccoons and opossums, interacted with top-notch wildlife biologists, and read a great deal of material in the area of my study.

A Career as a Field Biologist and Naturalist

I returned to India in the end of 1982. Daniel then appointed me the in-charge of the BNHS Project Elephant. Here I had two wonderful colleagues to work with, the late Ajay A. Desai and N. Sivaganesan. After initiating and making good progress with the project in the Mudumalai Wildlife Sanctuary, I left to join the newly established Wildlife Institute of India (WII) in Dehra Dun as a faculty in 1985.

With immense gratitude I would say that the golden period in my wildlife career started after I joined WII. The mandate of the WII was to train forest officers, both at the divisional forester and range forest officer levels; conduct research on various wildlife species and their habitats all across India; and create a cadre of young wildlife biologists through their master's program in wildlife science. I had wonderful colleagues in the Institute, the key person among them being G.S. Rawat, who hailed from the Himalayas. Interestingly, Rawat and I discovered the occurrence of the goral in the Rajaji National Park, and this was significant as the Uttar Pradesh forest department was of the opinion that there was no goral in the Park.

While with the WII, I had the opportunity to study various wildlife species such as the Asian elephant and lion, and ibex; and survey habitats of the tiger along the Himalayan foothills and of the Nilgiri tahr in the Western Ghats. Also, my interest in Jim Corbett made me go trekking to all the places where he had shot man-eating tigers and leopards. My research on various species, and the programs in WII gave me the opportunities to visit places in all the seven continents, including Alaska. I also wrote popular articles about the wildlife places I visited.

My Experiences in the Wild

My 45 years of experience in wildlife research and conservation has enabled me to record many interesting observations related to wildlife behaviour and conservation. I would like to share just a few of these.

What is it like inside a den? In the Sigur landscape I observed that striped hyenas carried their kills to their den where their young were left behind. Once Michael Fox and I crawled into a hyena den. We had a shield in front of our face fearing the attack of a porcupine which can also take shelter in the den. We discovered the interior to be very spacious where at least ten persons could crouch and sit. There were bones and skin of sambar deer. The den was full of fleas which crawled all over us, forcing us to rapidly crawl out of the den.

I have also had the chance to observe a pair of lions, in the late 1980s and early 1990s, when I was involved in a research on lions in the Gir forest. In the area near Sasan there were two males known as Dharam and Veer. They were the masters of a territory of about 150 sq km where there were two to three prides of females and young ones. We had radio-collared Dharam, and so we could follow the pair closely. Veer and Dharam found strength and courage in each other's company. They fought many battles with the adjacent male groups, and always won, with the loss only of some mane hair, and receiving some ghastly wounds which eventually healed. One day, in August 1987, Veer was killed by some local people. This had a disastrous effect on Dharam, who, brave till then, became a fugitive in his own home. He lost his mane, stopped roaring, and avoided cool valley habitats which were frequented by other males. He soon died of loneliness, fear and hunger. Ravi Chellam, the research scholar in this study, found Dharam's withered body reduced to a bag of bones.

And here is the case of an injured elephant. In mid-April 1990 a tusker from Rajaji National Park went out to feed in the agriculture landscape. In the ensuing man-animal conflict, a man was killed, and the villagers chased the tusker which took shelter in a sugar cane field. By this time the police had come on the scene, and, to placate the villagers, they fired some shots into the field. One bullet hit the right hind leg of the bull. The injured bull took asylum in the Rajaji National Park, and when I located him, accompanied by an armed guard, I found the wound had swollen to the size of an unhusked coconut, with blood and puss oozing out of it. The tusker was possibly forty-five years of age.

The bull allowed us to go as close to it as 15 to 20 feet, but when approached he always stood alert, cocking his ears, as if he was going to charge. The caring forest staff of the Park sprayed the wound with anti-infectant medicines and fly repellants, and placed antibiotics in sugar-coated *atta* balls for the elephant to eat. Also, plenty of sugar cane was given as food. In order to protect the bull from ivory poachers and other aggressive bulls, a few guards were stationed, who camped not far from the bull even at night with a camp fire going. Soon the wound started healing, and the tusker started to range around feeding and drinking from the pools. We heaved a sigh of relief thinking it was no longer needed to guard the bull. However, the bull's end came in an unexpected, tragic way. It got killed by another tusker one night in early May.

In the context of conservation there are issues around humans entering protected forest areas and national parks to collect forest produce. Poor village folk go into forests for collecting firewood, grass and medicinal plants. Of course, in a regulated way they should be monitored and allowed. But sadly, such people sometimes indulge in unlawful activities such as snaring for wildlife, and taking away kills of predators. In the early 1980s in the western part of Rajaji National Park (west of the Ganges River) there were at least 20 tigers. The prominent feature of this part of the Park is the Shivalik hills with an abundant growth of *bhabar* grass. The poor people from the villages on the border of the Park used to come to the hills in winter to cut the grass, and sell it for rope making.

The problem they caused was of stealing tiger and leopard kills, often a sambar. Even if it was a two-day-old kill they would take away the remains, as, in the freezing winter of the Shivaliks, the meat would not go bad. I myself witnessed 5 kills, of sambar, getting stolen this way.

Such stealing caused a loss of food for the tigers, and gradually led to the decline in their numbers so that some years ago only two old females were reported in the forests west of the Ganges. Now bhabar grass collection from the area has been totally stopped. And in 2020-'21 two tigers, a female and a male, were introduced in the western part of the Rajaji Tiger Reserve. Thanks to this there is a good potential for the tiger numbers to attain their former status within a decade or so.

I retired in 2005, and I am grateful to God that I am able to continue my conservation activities supported by organizations such as WWF-India, Nature Conservation Foundation and The Corbett Foundation. My sons, Mike and Mervin, are a great support in my conservation endeavours. My wanderings have also enabled me to write three popular books: *Field Days, A Naturalist's Journey through South and Southeast Asia*; *Walking the Western Ghats;* and *On Jim Corbett's Trail and Other Tales from the Jungle.*

❑❑❑